(3)

Siese
the moment!
God Bless!
Richard

Jim Nox

The Siege at Kekionga
Tecumseh's Uprising

Dedication

This book is dedicated to lifelong local fur trapper and cousin, Gary Pickett, and to all those who preserve our American and Native American Indian heritage.

Other books written by the Author

The Bones of Kekionga

The March to Kekionga

Author's Note

With really no intention to write a Kekionga series, the first book, *The Bones of Kekionga*, featuring General Josiah Harmar's campaign of 1790, was meant to be a one-and-done. Inspired partially by former students, I realized most people's knowledge of local and American history could use improvement. The thought that we may be walking, running, biking or driving by a spot where a Native American lived or took their last breath fighting for their homeland drove that truth home.

Hopefully in an exciting and adventurous way, our unique American history is brought to life on these pages to be appreciated.

The Siege at Kekionga
Tecumseh's Uprising

Jim Pickett

First Edition – 2021

OAK CREEK *media*

Bluffton, Indiana

Acknowledgements

I would like to recognize the places and people that made this story possible. A huge thank you goes to the following: Allen County Public Library and the helpful librarians who work there in Fort Wayne, IN; The History Center and all the great personnel employed there in Fort Wayne, IN; Historic Old Fort and all the great volunteers donating their time and talents, Fort Wayne, IN; Daughters of the American Revolution; Hanging Rock National Landmark, Lagro, IN; historical markers throughout Fort Wayne and the Midwest and the people who love our history that placed them there or gave permission to place a marker; Seven Pillars Nature Preserve, Peru, IN; Cincinnati Museum Center at Union Terminal; Fort Recovery State Museum; Andrew L. Tuttle Memorial Museum at Defiance, OH; Whitley County Historical Museum at Columbia City, IN; Tippecanoe Battlefield Museum, Battle Ground, IN; Prophetstown State Park in Tippecanoe County, IN; Wabash County Historical Museum and T.J. Honeycutt; Mississinewa Battlefield Society and its many great volunteers; and Historic Fort Wayne, Inc. Each of the places above have terrific people, and their facilities deserve a donation to keep our history alive.

A big thank you for information, advice and technical help goes to Mitch Harper; Jane Holliday (my wife); Bob Jones; Mike 'Chuck' Lake; Jed Pearson; Jacob Pickett; Stan Pickett; Rich Rozevink of Defiance, OH; Ed Schwartz, the publisher at Oak Creek Media, Bluffton, IN; and a special thank you to editor Melody Foreman, front cover design by Amber Steffen, the Wabash River and partial Northwest Territory map was produced by Aaron Steele, the 1808 ground plan of Fort Wayne is displayed with permission from The Allen County-Fort Wayne Historical Society.

Introduction

After "Mad" Anthony Wayne's fort was dedicated in October of 1794 at the confluence of the St. Marys and St. Joseph Rivers at an area known as Kekionga, 100 legion regulars under the command of Colonel John Hamtramck were left to defend it. The fort had been built on a rise overlooking the two rivers that formed the Maumee below it. Although crude in nature, it was a wooden and mostly earthen construction designed to withstand a British artillery bombardment. The first American fort was never in serious harm's way. It nonetheless stood in defiance of the Indians who had lived there for decades before and had resisted a 1790 American advancement led by General Josiah Harmar.

Anthony Wayne marched the rest of his legion back to his main wilderness headquarters at Fort Greeneville in the Ohio Territory and awaited leaders of those tribes he had invited to meet him there and negotiate a peace treaty. On August 3, 1795, the Treaty of Fort Greeneville opened up development of a portion of the Northwest Territory and ceded land to the United States that would eventually become parts of the states of Ohio, Indiana, Illinois and Michigan.

The treaty—negotiated by agents of the United States, General Anthony Wayne, William Henry Harrison and William Wells, who served as interpreter for the United States and for Chief Little Turtle, Blue Jacket, Tarhe, Leather Lips and other chiefs representing the Delaware, Miami, Ojibwa, Ottawa, Potawatomi, Shawnee and a Northwest Indian Confederation—signaled the end of formal hostilities between the two sides.

Relative peace existed around Fort Wayne over the next decade or so as the outpost on the western edge of the United States served as one of ten factories in the Northwest Territory that received trade items from the Indians, payed out annuities and supplied farming equipment to the natives in return for the land cessions made to the American government.

Colonel Thomas Hunt took over for Hamtramck as fort commander in 1798 and served until 1802. During his term, because of deteriorating conditions of the 1794 fort, a second Fort Wayne was built in 1800 down the hill and closer to the conjunction of the three rivers.

Several other commanders came and went in the early 1800s as a wild, untamed and rowdy community developed nearby.

As the first decade of the 19th century passed by, two revenge-seeking Shawnee brothers, Tecumseh and Tenskwatawa (later known as "The Prophet"), felt a calling to return the Indiana Territory if not Ohio to its rightful owners, the Native Americans.

The Siege at Kekionga: Tecumseh's Uprising serves as the third book in the Kekionga series, preceded by *The Bones of Kekionga* and *The March to Kekionga*. The author researched over fifty sources extensively in an attempt to create a flowing story that is easily understood. Over eighty percent of the people portrayed are real, and the rest are composites of people who would have existed.

Please find in the back of the book a list of all major and minor characters fictional and nonfictional that appeared in the three-book series.

Also, do not hesitate to use the map and an actual 1808 Fort Wayne ground plan to follow the historical fiction action.

As before, the author takes some liberty in utilizing the voices of those who were there and covers both the Indian and the American sides of the story. This book jumps 17 years ahead from *The March to Kekionga* that featured General Anthony Wayne and focuses on the time period of the summer of 1811 to September of 1812.

Now, prepare yourself to journey back to 1915, and then to 1811.

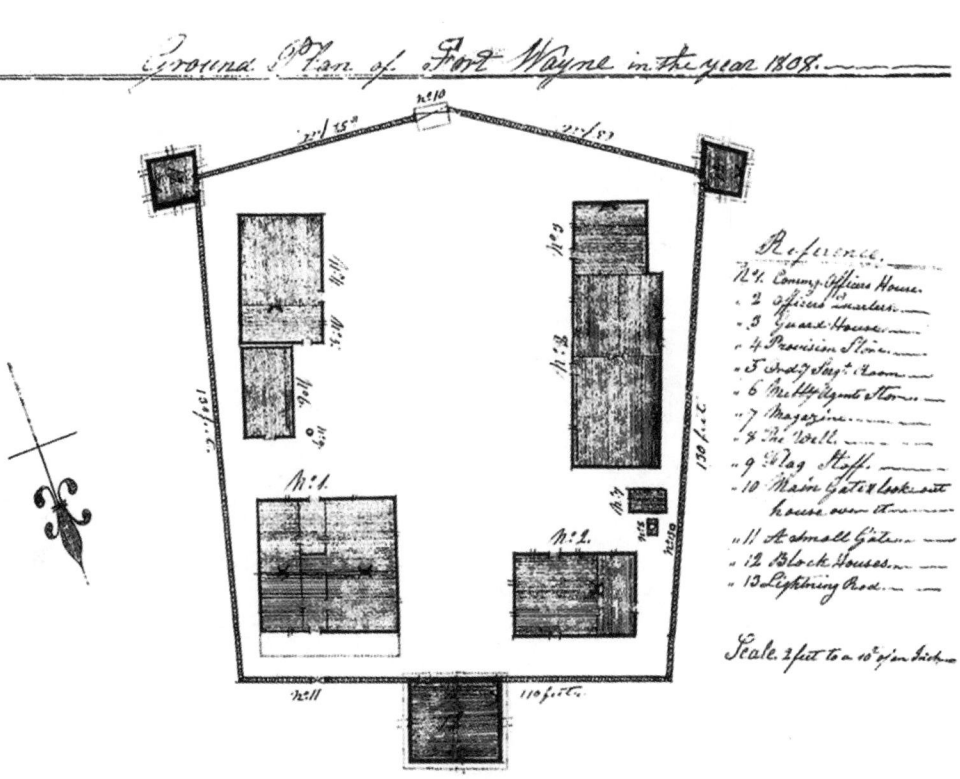

Ground Plan of Fort Wayne in the year 1808.

Reference.

Nº 1. Commg. Officer's House.
" 2. Officers Quarters.
" 3. Guard House.
" 4. Provision Store.
" 5. Ord.y Serg.t Room.
" 6. Mil.y Agents Store.
" 7. Magazine.
" 8. The Well.
" 9. Flag Staff.
" 10. Main Gate & look out
        house over the same.
" 11. A small Gate.
" 12. Block Houses.
" 13. Lightning Rod.

Scale 2 feet to a 10th of an inch.

Lake Michigan

Michigan Territory

Ft. Detroit

Malden

Lake Erie

Ft. Dearborn

Maumee River

St. Joe River

Tippecanoe River

Eel River

Little River

St. Mary's River

Ft. Defiance

Ft. Sandusky

Kekionga-Fort Wayne

Illinois Territory

Prophet's Town

Osage

Mississinewa River

Forks of the Wabash

St. Marys Oh.

Piqua

Ohio

Wabash River

Battle of Tippecanoe Nov. 7 1811

Indiana Territory

Ft. Greenville

Ft. Harrison

Ft. Washington

Vincennes

Ohio River

Frankfort Ky.

Kentucky

N
W   E
S

Wabash River

Forks of the Wabash

Little

Hanging Rock

Meto Cinnas Village

Wabash River

Salamonie River

Osage

Mississinewa River

Deaf Man's Village

Seven Pillars

Silver Heels Village

Battle of Mississinewa

Chapter 1

Late October 1915 — Old Fort Park, Fort Wayne, Indiana

"Dad burn, if I didn't get a chill all of a sudden!" comments Stan, a local construction worker.

"Yeah, the late-afternoon air can penetrate ya this time of year," replies his brother.

Tossing a nearby jacket to his sibling, he continues work removing concrete forms of a newly poured cement sidewalk at Old Fort Park in downtown Fort Wayne, Indiana, and placing the forms at a planned section to be constructed the next day.

"Well! Now, what do we have going on here?"

"Geez, Mr. Gavin! You just scared the daylights out of me!" states Stan.

"Sorry, friend," replies Gavin.

"What are you, part Indian? I didn't see you walking up through the park."

"If it isn't our local historian," chimes in Nyle, with a smile.

"Ha! I thought you two boys were coal deliverers?" asks Gavin.

"Only part-time when they need us, and we'll probably be doing that after we get this job done remodeling the park," responds Stan while lifting up his end of a 12-foot-long two-by-four. "In fact, Nyle and I will be applying for a job at the telephone company."

"Ah yes, a worthy profession in this day and age," reacts Gavin. "I'll still be seeing you guys around once in a while, I'm sure, but I'll never forget accidently scaring those undertakers carrying the skulls that you found in Mrs. Harrington's basement. You boys have a tendency to discover some interesting items."

"Well don't look now, but we uncovered some old pioneer graves over on the northwest side of this park," informs Stan while pointing past the pedestalled Spanish cannon and children's swing set. "See those three piles of dirt over by that policeman?"

"Well, I'll be!" exclaims Bob Gavin. "Ya did it again?"

"Oh you missed all the excitement. Quite a spectacle for a while until they covered up the deceased with a tarp," says Nyle, walking back from the construction truck with a jacket for himself. "Undertaker people are coming later today to remove them."

"Seems like ever since Little Turtle's grave was found at Dr. Gillie's home on Lawton Place Avenue three years ago, folks are always looking for something old and valuable," comments Gavin.

"Hey, I got a question for you, Mr. Gavin," Stan says, pulling his sock hat over his ears. "I thought you told us the old military Fort Wayne was south of here up that hill where the rock is on Berry and Clay streets. They even have a plaque stating that. Why then do they call this area here Old Fort Park?"

"Oh, you mean I never told you? Dad burn! There were two other American forts right here where you boys are working."

"Two others?" Nyle responds, shaking his head while grabbing a shovel to backfill the finished sidewalk. "Why'd they need two more?"

The elderly retired amateur historian eagerly explains, "Most of the forts back then were made of wood, and it would weaken and rot away. The Americans built the second one in 1800 or thereabouts and the third one about 1815 or '16. I forget."

"I'm no military guy," states Stan, "but looks like they wanted to get closer to the rivers for drinking water and such but they gave up the defensive high ground in doing that."

"Oh, I think it about came back to haunt them during the siege," answers Mr. Gavin, his voice trailing away.

"The Siege? Man, it just keeps getting richer," Nyle says in wonderment. "This is all very interesting, Mr. Gavin, but Stan and I hav'ta finish up here for the day before it gets dark."

"Yep, yep, yep, I understand. I get a little historically carried away sometimes. Ha! Good talking to you guys. I have to leave anyway. We'll finish this discussion some other day," says Gavin, waving and crossing the Clay Street railroad tracks and heading for the Columbia Avenue Bridge. "And by the way," he yells back, "the old Wabash and Erie Canal use to pass through where these railroad tracks are."

"Wabash and Erie Canal passed through there? No way, Mr. Gavin!"

"Calm down, Stan, or he'll never leave," urges Nyle.

"That's another one for another day!" asserts Bob Gavin as he waves, walking toward the bridge. "And by the way, I'm heading toward the Kekionga orchard!"

"What did he say?" asks Stan.

"Never mind, brother."

As the coworkers hustle to make up for lost time talking to Gavin, minutes pass by and more forms for tomorrow's concrete job dominate the brothers' attention. Suddenly, Nyle receives a chill from a hand touching his shoulder.

"Dad gum, where'd that iciness come from?" he asks without looking up. "You need to put some gloves on, Mr. Gavin. And I thought you left?"

"Ah, ahhh, it's not Mr. Gavin, Nyle," discloses Stan, facing upward at a middle-aged man dressed in a navy blue military uniform and holding a dark shako hat under his arm.

Nyle, staring at the stranger's well-worn shoes, slowly elevates his eyes and asks, "Can we help you, mister?"

"Where's the fort?" curtly questions the stranger, gazing around.

"Well, the fort's been gone for about a hundred years, but if you're looking for the graves," answers Nyle, not waiting for a response, "they are over by that policeman."

As the man walks away, Nyle bends down to adjust a form and says, "Come on, Stan, we gotta finish this. Sue is expecting me home for supper on time for a change."

Now standing, Stan reacts, "That's weird. The uniformed guy just here and walking toward the policeman just vanished."

"Who vanished?" asks Nyle, gathering to his feet.

Staring at where the man had been walking fifty yards away, his brother replies, "The name embroidered on his uniform jacket read Lieutenant Philip Ostrander."

"Ostrander? Well, he must have stooped down to get something off the ground," reasons Nyle.

"I wonder why he is dressed in that old uniform and what his story is?" queries Stan, staring at where the missing soldier was.

Chapter 2

"You should have your thumbs cut off! Every one of you!" shouts the visiting, muscular 43-year-old Shawnee war Chief Tecumseh in Algonquin. "All of you who have signed these so-called peace treaties with the Americans have foolishly given away our land. It is time to take it back!"

The hundred listeners gathered circularly under an expansive elm tree along the St. Joseph River wait silently and intently for his next words.

"What did you get in return from these white devils?"

Not waiting for an answer from Little Turtle, chiefs Richardville and Le Gris, or braves of all ages, Tecumseh raises his voice even further, "Whiskey, farming supplies and money to buy these so-called domestic tools? Did you not get guns and ammunition? I bet not. The whites are afraid you will use them on them when you figure out how foolish you have been!"

Sitting on the perimeter of the Indian inner circle are 17-year-olds Red Hawk, the son of Running Deer and Morning Bird, and Wayne Pastor Carlisle, one of only two whites present at the assembly. Both boys were born during General Anthony Wayne's short two-month stay at Fort Wayne while it was being built three miles south of this powwow. The young men are beginning to feel guilty even though they had no part of any peace treaty.

"What unrest do you continue to bring to our villages along the three rivers of our communities?" speaks 60-year-old Chief Little Turtle, the longtime war chief of the Miami Nation, struggling to get to his feet to challenge the main speaker.

"Sit back down, Little Turtle," commands Tecumseh, "your generation has come and gone. Yes, you had your great victories against La Balme on the Eel River, here at the Battle of Kekionga and at the upper Wabash against St. Clair, but you did not act alone. There were many tribes and chiefs that worked together. You get all the glory because of your sound piece sitting next to you, William Wells."

Ignoring Tecumseh's disrespect, The Turtle rises to his feet and rebuts the Shawnee chief, "We have had many years of peace with the Americans since the last battle at Fallen Timbers. There is no need for further bloodshed. I have seen the many towns and cities these American's live in when I went east of the Appalachians with my friend and still considered son-in-law, Captain Wells. He is a trusted interpreter of the multiple languages he understands."

"Ah, you are a fool to believe him," counters Tecumseh.

Assertively cutting off Tecumseh, Little Turtle continues, "The Americans have as many people as the stars in the sky. They will not stop coming to our land even when defeated."

Pacing around the center fire, Tecumseh responds, "I do not trust the words of a man who has given away our land, and I surely do not trust this William Wells whom you have confidence in. He once fought with us and then he spied and fought against us! No, we need many warriors from all across our native land from Ohio to the Mississippi River and from Mackinaw and the Great Lakes to the southern boundaries of the Choctaw and Chickasaw in the south!"

Nudging the elbow of his lifetime friend Red Hawk, Wayne Pastor nods his head affirmatively as he stares at the bulging neck and facial muscles of the great Indian orator chief that stands above him.

Red Hawk glances back at the boy he considers his blood brother and instinctively knows what he is thinking. The two have heard Tecumseh and other chiefs before who agree with him, and have seen firsthand how the whites have controlled the Native American land.

"My brother, The Prophet, has many visions. You remember the total solar eclipse he predicted and how amazingly that came true? But the one that continues to stir his soul is the glorious victory and re-attainment of our land. So convinced of our Native American unity to come, my brother and I have moved from Chillicothe on the Scioto River to Prophetstown on the Wabash River in what the Americans call the

Indiana Territory. The Americans and this untrustworthy white man named William Henry Harrison cannot stop us!"

"Hold on, Tecumseh," speaks Miami Chief Richardville, the nephew of Little Turtle. "I have not seen these huge American villages that Little Turtle tells us of, but after we defeated the Americans on the upper Wabash, the invaders came back with Wayne, the leader who never slept, and ended up building the last of his many forts right here at Kekionga."

"I would think you would be one of the first to raise his tomahawk, Richardville, especially after the whites took away the portage from you and your mother, Tah Cum Wah," retorts Tecumseh. "Ah, you give up too easily. We need warriors of the new generation to join me and our brothers that are already with The Prophet, where the Tippecanoe River meets the Wabash! And I must add, our fathers, the British, have resolved to support us with cannon to knock down the walls of these American forts!"

Riding horseback slowly north on their American government-supported scouting route are E.J. Carlisle and his once-enemy at the Battle of Kekionga and now-Miami Indian friend Running Deer. Unaware but following rumors of Tecumseh holding a meeting somewhere in the surrounding area, thoughts about their sons dictate their conversation.

"I took Red Hawk on a trip to some of his ancestral land along the Wabash and Mississinewa rivers earlier this summer, as you know," says Running Deer. "He is a man. He hunts and fishes well. Can handle a bow equally as well as a musket. He can live in the wilderness, and back in the day, he would have performed gallantly against all enemies. But he is restless, much like we were at our sons' age. During a short stay in a Miami village, he met an Indian maiden and they fell in love."

"I have seen similar things in Wayne Pastor," states the weather-worn veteran frontiersman riding alongside Running Deer. "On our trip down the Maumee to old Fort Defiance and beyond to the rapids last spring, he also showed the skills of the river, camping and hunting."

Alerted by a loud dispute, the two pull up 100 yards from the Tecumseh gathering, dismount their horses, and watch the proceedings through bushes located under a honey locust tree.

"Looks like Tecumseh means business, Running Deer."

"He and his brother have meant business that has been growing more rapidly the last couple years, E.J. If Governor Harrison doesn't understand that now, he soon will."

"Yep. I don't enjoy the looks I've been getting lately from the younger natives whenever I pass by them at the fort and in Frenchtown."

After a while, the two scouts notice the parley breaking up, mount their horses and ride toward the departing assembly. Largely ignored by the Indians leaving the site, their two sons walk toward them with glaring disapproval.

"Spying on us, huh?" asks Wayne Pastor in perfect Algonquin language.

"Yes, my father, were you too afraid to come forward?" quizzes Red Hawk. "The great Tecumseh can be very intimidating. Can he not?"

"The Chief speaks of war, Red Hawk." Sternly staring and not liking to be challenged, Running Deer continues, "Shall I show you the graves of both the whites and our people? Shall I uncover the dirt they are buried under to show you the horror of how they died?"

"You sound like Little Turtle, the old warrior of long ago. This is a new time. A new opportunity to gain our land back," insists Red Hawk.

"I see an injustice, Dad, that can be rectified," agrees Wayne Pastor in English, looking at E.J.

"I don't know where you're getting these fancy words, son. Must be the education your mother has given you and your younger siblings, but she is not going to be happy about these ideas you're coming up with, and to be honest neither am I," speaks E.J., a veteran of three campaigns that began in 1790. "Your Great-Uncle Isaac, as you well know, lost his whole family back in Pennsylvania to the enemy you're thinking of joining up with."

"Not thinking about, father. Red Hawk and I are leaving tomorrow for Prophetstown. Our family should have never come to this side of the Appalachians," informs Wayne Pastor. "I will be changing my name, as well. I cannot live up to this so-called American hero General 'Mad' Anthony Wayne. And I'm not sure this Pastor you and mom tell me about and named me after would worship a God that would allow the Native Americans to be rooted from their land!"

The four stare at each other for a moment.

"You know what this means, don't you, Red Hawk, my beloved eldest son?" reasons an alarmed and downtrodden Running Deer. "We may find ourselves fighting against each other in battle someday."

"I think the Great Manitou will not allow that to happen if your personal manitou guides you correctly. Only the future knows what will happen. Hopefully," finishes Red Hawk, "you will choose the correct side."

The next morning, after quietly gathering their belongings the night before and avoiding a confrontation with their mothers that was sure to bring great sorrow, Red Hawk and Wayne Pastor put their things inside a canoe, which they lift and carry on their shoulders westerly along the tree-lined narrow portage trail that runs parallel to the St. Marys River on their left. Midsummer drought conditions make navigation to the normal beginning carrying place impossible. Two miles further, where the two most common portage trails converge west of Kekionga, a familiar face appears.

"Well now, you boys coming to earn a little more cash?" greets the smiling portage manager businessman, Louis Bourie.

"Actually, Mr. Bourie, Red Hawk and I are passing through and are going to save us a little money and transport ourselves. With the water being so low, what do you think? Eight miles till we get to the Little Wabash?"

"Oh, I would say farther than eight for sure," responds Bourie in his broken French and English. "Once you get to the put-in, it should be smooth sailing all the way to the Gulf of Mexico. Ha! Going on a little trip are you?"

"Heading down the Wabash, Mr. Bourie, and let me ask you, don't you feel guilty about conducting business on this passageway being as my people were here first many decades ago?" asks Red Hawk.

Not smiling anymore, Bourie speaks, "I sense the same stirrings I am witnessing traveling through here. Be careful what you're doing, you two. As many Miami are content with the peace as there are with your sentiments. There is trouble brewing, and not just with the disenchanted warriors passing by, but the British are showing much arrogance. I'll tell ya what fellows, let me show you my gratitude for all the packhorses you've led. Your loyalty has made me a lot of money the last few years. Take a couple of my best packhorses at no charge and just tie them up at the other end. You know where I mean. My wife, Spotted Fawn, is waiting there with some of your fellow coworkers to help an expected Antoine Bondie's return."

"We appreciate the offer and the money you have paid us in the past, but we are men," responds Wayne Pastor. "Also, my name is now White Snake."

Bourie slowly shakes his head and watches the two young men lift their birch-bark canoe full of their belongings up on their shoulders and begin walking the wagon-rutted, tree-lined trail to the put-in place of the Little Wabash River.

A couple hours later at the top of the highest point of the portage, the boys set their canoe down to take a break and let packhorse-led traders pass by.

"Well, I kind of feel a little foolish not allowing Bourie to loan us the packhorses," states White Snake. "This is a little tougher than leading packhorses."

"We'll learn not to be so self-reliant as we go. Just keep our cause in mind," offers Red Hawk, this time in English. "All right, let's go. It's just a bit farther."

Upon reaching the narrow but 7-foot-deep put-in place, the two wave at Spotted Fawn, secure their supplies and shove off paddling, having their flintlock rifles at their ready.

"You know, Red Hawk, Malden, up by Fort Detroit, perhaps would have been closer. Most of the Miami sympathizing with Tecumseh are heading that way from Kekionga to connect with the British."

"I am aware, White Snake," says Red hawk still getting use to his friend's new name, "but The Prophet is this way, and the movement begins with him and Tecumseh. We have the weapons already. We don't need the British supplies just yet."

Besides, there is another reason," continues Red Hawk, smoothly dipping his oar into the channel. "A beautiful young lady named Wy-nu-sa awaits me just beyond the Forks of the Wabash. I met her earlier this year, and we're in love."

As the friends navigate a bend in the 10-foot-wide, gently moving current, two young bear cubs drinking and splashing in the water suddenly appear ahead.

"Whoa! Back-paddle, Wayne Pastor, back-paddle! Watch for the mama bear!"

Both young men jam their flat paddle into the water to slow the rapidly-moving canoe, but the warning is warranted as the protective mother charges out of the forest, bounds down the bank through the tall weeds, running and growling at the two humans approaching her cubs. Leaping toward the canoe with extended claws, a single talon from her right paw snags the pointed stern and tips the canoe violently. With a huge splash, the bear submerges. "Go! Go! Go! Go forward Red Hawk!" shouts a panicking White Snake, now soaked along with some supplies.

As the mother bear leaps and swims frantically toward the pals, more orders are bellowed. "Fast forward, yell at those cubs, Red Hawk! Get it going! Mama's gaining on us!"

"Yaaaa! Yaaaa!" The two holler, furiously dipping deeply into the narrow river and moving directly at the cubs to scare them out of the water and out of their way. "Yaaaa! Keep it going! Ha!" laughs Wayne

Pastor, watching the scrambling frightened cubs clamoring up the banks and sensing the relief of a close-call escape.

"There better not be their daddy nearby, or we're in trouble again!" warns a smiling but observant Red Hawk.

After pulling away from the sow and past the frightened bear cubs, the two glance back from 50 yards downstream and coast a bit to catch their breath.

"You were telling about this girlfriend that awaits you, Red Hawk?" utters a grinning White Snake.

"One of the prettiest Miami girls I've ever met," says a blushing and smiling Red Hawk. "It's hard to believe she would like someone like me."

"River is widening. I think the beavers have jammed up things with a dam," reasons White Snake. "What you say we pull over here, carry our canoe around and camp for the night?"

"Ok, it's a little swampy, but we can find some high ground to sleep."

Chapter 3

Late Summer 1811 — Fort Wayne/Indiana Territory

"I'll tell you what, Commander Rhea," advises Toussaint Dubois, scout and special representative of Governor William Henry Harrison, "I know he needs punished, but give this Private Jennings a break. We need these Indian chiefs coming in to have a good feeling about Fort Wayne."

"Lieutenant Ostrander and I will take it under advisement, Dubois," says Fort Wayne commander Captain James Rhea, as he and Dubois exit the 6-foot-3-inch-wide main gate under Fort Wayne's lookout house walking south and making a right turn toward the supply factory.

Dubois shakes his head and expresses, "One hundred lashes on a bare back and then six days of hard labor with a ball and chain tied to his ankle? A little harsh, don't you think?"

"Hey, Dubois, you are a French trader from Vincennes. You've never commanded a fort. The constant stealing, fighting, drunkenness goes on and on. I have to do something to keep some order around here."

"And you, Captain Rhea, have never tossed a few whiskeys?" argues Dubois. "It gets a little boring in the wilderness after years of peace, but after talking to those eleven chiefs, your men may get tested soon."

"Come on," replies Rhea, "they're not serious. It wasn't long ago that William Wells thought Fort Wayne would be abandoned like Fort Defiance was. What ya say we inform agent Johnston what the chiefs informed us? Let's go this way. He should be in the factory."

"Man, there's dozens of folks around today," notices Dubois, as the drum and fife instrumentalists parade the grounds, entertaining the noontime crowd.

Seeing the men walking side by side with a military escort that joined them, toward the Indian agent's factory building 100 yards west of the wall of Fort Wayne, assistant agent William Oliver anxiously departs the factory and, meandering through the crowd of frontiersmen and Indians, greets Dubois and Commander Rhea.

"What'd those chiefs say?" asks Oliver. "They going to war?"

"Half no, half wouldn't commit either way," expresses Dubois. "I think they are afraid of Tecumseh. Where's John Johnston?"

"Inside, probably wishing he were somewhere else. The usual Indians are awaiting their ration of whiskey and the trading of their animal hides for a fair amount of cash. The annuities are running a little late, so that is an issue, Dubois. You can pass that along to Governor Harrison. I'll go back in and relieve Johnston so you can talk to him personally."

Meanwhile, nearby, a group of veterans of the Indian wars and longtime occupants of Kekionga notice Dubois.

"Well now, look what we have here, fellas," expresses Private John Smith, a military messenger and scout.

"Who-whee! Give this Dubois a drink. He looks mighty thirsty!" chides French trader and longtime Kekionga resident Antoine Lasselle. "And don't tell me you had a close call with those chiefs during that council meeting inside those fort walls."

"Close call? I'll show you what a close call is," says William Wells, as the former Indian agent for ten years at Fort Wayne holds up his useless left wrist with his right hand. "I about got killed scouting for Anthony Wayne back in '94."

"That was when you and old Mac McMahon got overconfident with those Delaware, wasn't it?" interrupts farmer and current U.S. government scout E.J. Carlisle, listening from outside the circle.

"Mac? There's a guy who could jump!" Wells continues. "Why, he jumped over the back of his horse, mounting it, as we were getting away from those angry rascals!"

"Jump? Why I saw him leap clear over a team of moving horses while they were pulling a wagon! Ha!" laughs E.J. "Made me some money wagerin' on that."

"You and that old hoot, Mike Fink, the Ohio River king," adds Private John Smith. "Mac and Fink could do the craziest tricks, and I never saw a bet they couldn't win."

"Close call my butt, Wells!" says Lasselle, finally getting a word in. "Wayne about hung me at Fallen Timbers for allegedly fighting alongside the Indians." Clasping his neck with his hands, he further explains, "I was this close to hanging from that old cottonwood tree growing along the Maumee bank next to Fort Miami! Those dad burn British scalawags wouldn't help me."

"They ought to hang you anyways for all the cheating you been doing trading with us folks. Ha!" says a laughing Dubois.

"And scalp you ta boot, while you's a hangin'!" chips in Smith.

"Little Turtle would like to end my life, too! Ha!" spouts a laughing Lasselle, crossing his eyes. "Although, I can never tell when he is joking! Ha! That would be a grand ending tale, wouldn't it? Kilt by the living legend himself, The Turtle! Where is he, by the way? I haven't seen him for a while."

"He's living at his birth home area near the Blue River or the Eel. Not exactly sure," informs Captain Rhea.

"Ah, you boys don't know what close is," says a suddenly serious Private Smith, not smiling. "It was on down the Maumee on the south bank of the river on the other side of the fort. I laid all day and night with an injured leg that got shot during the attack into Kekionga back in 1790. All the while, I was praying hard that the Indians wouldn't spot me before the Americans found me."

"Tell 'em what was goin' on, Smitty," requests E.J., already familiar with Smith's close calls.

"Well, I had to watch while hidden behind a log as the injuns busted up the bodies and stole the clothing of my fallen fellow soldieries." Lifting his arm and pointing up the hill to the south, Smith somberly finishes, "Those guys are buried on the hill west of the first Fort Wayne."

William Wells breaks the sudden solemnity and suggests, "Hey fellas, let's go pester Ike Carlisle at his sutlery shop and move away from this cheatin' Indian agent Johnston coming this way. Let's go discuss how high we're going to hang that British Indian agent Alexander McKee when we catch him for stirring up our Indian friends."

Two hundred miles to the southwest of Fort Wayne on the Wabash River at Vincennes, the capital of the Indiana Territory, Governor William Henry Harrison anxiously awaits the Fort Wayne news from Toussaint Dubois.

"Mr. Dubois will be our lead scout and should arrive from the outpost at Kekionga any day now, Colonel Boyd. Are your troops settled in ok around Grouseland?" asks Harrison.

"I think so."

"Meantime, we can plan our approach to Prophetstown," says Governor Harrison, pacing the floor of the parlor room at his personal mansion.

"Yes, yes, that would be good," remarks the yawning officer, who brought 350 members of his 4TH U.S. Regiment from Pittsburg to fight the Tecumseh coalition.

"I understand this can seem boring after spending 20 years helping to lead 150,000 troops including a 500-elephant cavalry in India," snarks Harrison, "but I have more than once seen peace delegates enter into the wilderness to seek peace among these aborigines. Unfortunately, they do not come back alive or, occasionally, in one piece. So this is serious business. Do you understand?"

"Of course, Governor," answers a derogatory Boyd, looking at the American military general who has never led an army into combat before.

"I'll add one more thing, Colonel, and you too, Aide-de-camp Owen," informs Harrison, staring out the front window. "This comet that we see blazing across the night sky just gives The Prophet more credence and the warriors he commands increased boldness."

"I agree," says Owen. "That solar eclipse he predicted gave the Indian movement momentum, as if the Treaty of Fort Wayne wasn't enough incentive."

"Hey, that was a fair exchange of terms that all the chiefs agreed to and signed," reasons a defensive Harrison.

"Except Tecumseh and The Prophet," counters Owen.

"I have met with Tecumseh twice. One time he wants peace, the next time he wants war. Besides, they are from the Ohio country and have no legal bearings on Indiana. Now let's move on. With the troops Colonel Boyd has brought us to join the 85 from Kentucky and the 490 militia from Knox, Harrison and Clark counties here in Indiana, we have swelled our army to close to 1000 men, including officers."

"The army muskets of 1795 and bayonets have been distributed," condenses Owen. "More ammunition, powder, flour sacks for bread and cattle to be butchered on the way to Prophetstown to feed this army are on the way, sir."

"Don't forget the contractors to build the boats to take this army up the Wabash," adds Harrison. "You see, John. May I call you that, Colonel Boyd?"

"If you wish."

"This mission has two objectives, and interject if you wish, John. Before I tell you them, let's take a look at this map," directs Harrison, unrolling a large sketch on the parlor center table. "We need to move the army up the Wabash about sixty miles and build a defensive fort to protect Vincennes. From there, we will again head up the Wabash, by boat this time, toward Prophetstown. Then by land, cross the prairie to surprise the rascals near the Tippecanoe River."

"These objectives you speak of are what?" inquires Colonel Boyd.

"President Madison has his hands full with the British and doesn't need the Indians helping them, Colonel Boyd," advises Harrison, "so we need to disperse the Indians from Prophetstown and dissuade them from joining Tecumseh. Disperse and dissuade."

"Last we heard, Tecumseh was traveling south into Alabama to recruit the Chocktaw, Chickasaw and Creek," apprises Colonel Owen.

"They've been enemies of Tecumseh over the years, have they not?" asks the now engaged Boyd.

"Yes, but since 1797, there has been a truce between them," informs Harrison. "I find it hard to believe that fighting alongside century-old adversaries will happen, but one never knows. Listen to me clearly! While Tecumseh is away, we need to strike."

Gazing into the Fort Wayne sky, the silence is broken. "That comet is beautiful, isn't it, Charlotte?" asks E.J. Carlisle to his wife on the front steps of their farm cabin 1000 yards west of Fort Wayne.

"I can't help but wonder if Wayne Pastor is watching it too?" says Charlotte.

"Yes, I wouldn't doubt it. But I know what you're going to say, and you know the answer, Charlotte."

"But dad burnit, E.J.! You and—"

"Settle down, now. You've been hangin' around that fort too much, Charlotte. Don't be swearin' like that. Besides, the kids are tryin' to sleep," admonishes E.J.

"You and Running Deer should follow those boys down that Wabash and bring them back!"

"They are not boys anymore, Charlotte. You remember when Uncle Isaac allowed me to tag along with him and join the Pennsylvania militia to help General Harmar's army twenty-one years ago?"

"That was different. You had your uncle with you."

"You forget Bobby and Ben were my age then, and they didn't have chaperones."

"E.J., after a bit, they had Uncle Isaac looking after them, too, and you know it!" says Charlotte, beginning to tear up. "And you also know what happened to Ben? He's buried up on the hill, and you know what happened to my family except for Phillip and me. I just can't stand the thought of Wayne Pastor ending up like that, only this time at the very hands of the country we work for and are citizens of."

"I'll talk to Running Deer, but I think he'll agree that it's just like when Bobby, Ben, Uncle Isaac and I came out here to homestead. We had a purpose and cause, and so does our son and Red Hawk. To be honest, I can see both sides of this situation. God willing, they both will be back with us unharmed."

A couple days later, Running Deer and E.J. are patrolling several miles east of Fort Wayne near the Maumee River.

"Whaaa! Wooo, wooo, ah, ah! Oh, I think he got me! Ow!"

"What's goin' on, mister?" asks E.J. "You ok, and what are you doin' jumpin' around like a loony bird?"

"Yellow jacket just went up my pant leg, and he stung me. I'll bring him out real slow," informs the baggy-clothed loner that seemed to appear out of nowhere along the south trail parallel to the Maumee. "I don't want to harm him. He didn't know any better. I got into his domain, and he got frightened."

"Now be careful, stranger," warns Running Deer, staring down from his horse. "He'll sting you again."

"Oh, I'll be careful. I love nature. Everything on this earth has a purpose. There, now," says the long-billed capped naturalist as he works the yellow jacket toward the bottom of his frayed, oversized pant leg and out the bottom next to his shoeless feet.

"Where did you come from?" asks E.J. "I haven't ever seen you out this way before, although I think I have heard some Indian rumors about a white man that had come along."

"Came from Massachusetts originally with my brother Nathan," speaks the peculiar man, placing cold, wet mud on the sting up his pant leg, "but he settled down in Ohio. I'll go visit him before winter sets in and get some more seeds from the cider factories in Pennsylvania before I come back this way next spring. I kinda like it out here. The land's level and real fertile."

"Sorry, mister, we didn't introduce ourselves, but I'm E.J. and this is Running Deer."

"Chapman's my name. Just call me John if you wish."

"You have a shed or cabin?" asks Running Deer. "Do you have a horse?"

"My old horse is over there grazing in that small meadow. He carries my bag of seed and my needs. I sleep under the stars or in a tree. There's been folks that take me in occasionally. I hear there is a fort nearby. The Indians have been real kind to me, but I have to admit, they are not too fond of that garrison being at a place called Kekionga."

"Well, it's been a shame peace couldn't come before it had to be built," says a sympathizing E.J.

"What is your purpose, Chapman? You will not stay the winter?" asks Running Deer.

"All I have to do is plant 50 apple trees and 20 peach and stay on this land for three years, and the land speculators will give me 100 acres. I have to clear it off somewhat. I've planted some trees over in Ohio that some nice folks are watching for me. Then I'll probably sell the 100 acres to new homesteaders to buy more seed."

"Hmmm. Running Deer or I can probably oversee this land for you, and perhaps my wife, Charlotte, and I may buy some from you if ever the animosity with the Indians settles down."

"Well, you two comrades seem to get along ok, and I've found the Indians nearby here real friendly. Personally, I don't seem to have any problem with any folks. I just love the Lord and the Lord's land and blend in."

"What do you think, Running Deer?" asks E.J.

"There is a lot of potential out here," answers Running Deer. "I'll talk it over with Morning Bird and see what she has to say."

"I'm a little afraid to bring Charlotte outside the square mile around the fort, let alone the thirty-six square miles the government has set aside around Fort Wayne according to the Indian peace treaty, but Mr. Chapman, let's..." halts E.J. midsentence. "Now where did he go?"

Running Deer surveys the surrounding area and says in wonderment, "His horse is gone too."

Chapter 4

Summer into Winter 1811 — Wabash River/Mississinewa River/Fort Wayne area of the Indiana Territory

"It is good that you two got here when you did, Red Hawk. Your friend's poisonous bite had him in trouble," says Pechewa, part-time resident of the Forks of the Wabash.

"All we were doing was gathering some firewood near a log jam the beavers had created on the Little Wabash, when the massasauga bit him on the hand."

"It is fortunate you received help from the herbalists rather than the ones who would rely on our shaman."

"I usually carry the black cohosh in my deerskin pouch," explains Red Hawk. "I guess I forgot during the excitement of leaving Kekionga."

"Why not stay at The Forks a bit longer and let E.J.'s son recover a few days more? Perhaps you want to settle here? There is plentiful hunting, fishing and trading with the French who live here or journey through."

"We have appreciated the hospitality White Snake and I have received, but we are joining The Prophet," answers Running Deer in the native Algonquin language.

"Ah, yes, the Shawnee chief who has the visions and his warrior sibling, Tecumseh. I have seen a few braves, and not just Miami, passing through. Trouble looms with those Shawnee brothers."

Not wanting to hear another lecture, "It is time for us to go," says the snake-bit Wayne Pastor, now known as White Snake, finishing his cornbread and squash furnished by a sub-chief's daughter. "I can finish my body painting later."

"You look Miami, White Snake; the transition is taking place," compliments Red Hawk.

"You have much more to learn, young brothers," advises Pechewa. "Some of the Miami villages up ahead have different beliefs."

Ignoring the elder Indian, White Snake addresses Red Hawk. "The transition began many years ago, my friend. It is now the time to move forward, although I don't think I can wear the breechcloth like you do."

"Don't worry about that," comforts Red Hawk, "the leather moccasins, leggings and beaded headband are fine, and you learn quick about the paint markings and symbolism. Those things are meaningful, but mentally and emotionally you are becoming your own brave."

"Sorry to see you two move on," says Pechewa. "The time you have spent here has seen the healing you need, White Snake. Red Hawk, it is always good to see clan again. Harmar's invasion, followed by St. Clair and then 'the one who never sleeps' has scattered us. Tell your father, Running Deer, and mother, Morning Bird, aya."

With a canoe half full of hides obtained during the stay at the Forks of the Wabash, food and a few weapon supplies, the young companions ply the Wabash River southwesterly for two hours when they spot several deer heads breaking the surface of the water 200 yards ahead.

"They are staying cool from this unusually warm weather. Let's drift to the left slowly and get within range before they realize we are not a log," suggests Red Hawk while deftly grabbing his musket.

Moments silently pass by when Red Hawk suddenly directs, "Ok, they spot us. Let's get with the current, and I will take the large racked buck as he ascends the bank. Steady now."

Aiming his musket rifle and waiting for just the right moment, Red Hawk eyes the emerging whitetail deer and gently squeezes the trigger.

BAM!

Red Hawk raises his head above the puff of musket smoke to catch a glimpse of his target.

"He's down," advises White Snake, who has the better view.

Paddling forward to claim their game, Red Hawk reasons, "It is good to have our own food and not rely on each village to take us in. The deer hide will be helpful at the next village we come to. If I remember right from my trip with my father earlier this year, ah yes. Look past the deer that I regretfully had to shoot. You can barely make it out. The hanging rock that protrudes well above the bank is very unique and is a good marker to gain your bearings on this river."

Spotting the ancient limestone protrusion on the south side of the waterway, White Snake reacts. "I see it. I think there is someone on top."

"It is flat up there, perhaps 75 feet from the surface of the river this time of year. Small ceremonies take place at the crest as well as scouting observations. One can see distances quite far up and down the river."

"I am sure we have been seen, Red Hawk."

"More than that, White Snake. I will be seeing the love of my life again. Wy-nu-sa's village is not far from the rock."

The next day, the two Miami canoe toward Wy-nu-sa's village and ram the canoe into the riverbank to disembark.

"Salutation et bienvenue! Bonjure!" comes a greeting from two approaching wide-armed Jesuit priest missionaries in their cassocks and three-piece birettas on their heads. "Let us help carry your hides that you wish to trade."

"Thank you," speaks Red Hawk in French. "What is the going rate?" "One hundred cents per deer hide, don't let them cheat you," smiles the missionary, holding his hand to the side of his mouth.

"Let's finish this up and find Wy-nu-sa," says Red Hawk.

"Lead the way," complies White Snake.

Entering the village, Red Hawk eagerly informs his companion, "Wy-nu-sa lost her father at the Battle of Fallen Timbers, and her mother, now quite elderly, was pregnant with her when he died. Oh, there she is by the sprawling oak tree," he says, waving to gain her attention.

Wy-nu-sa notices him and walks toward the young braves from Kekionga.

"Wy-nu-sa!" yells Red Hawk.

"Easy, my friend," whispers White Snake. "Who is that warrior with her?"

Slightly lifting her buckskin dress to jog toward Red Hawk, the young maiden smiles and then stops to look back at her slowly following companion.

"It is so good to see you again," says Wy-nu-sa, staring and walking again toward Red Hawk until she falls into an embrace with him and gives a short kiss on his cheek.

"My love, my darling," says Red Hawk, noticing a slight draw back. "What is it, my beloved? I told you I would be back."

"Red Hawk, I want you to meet Big Elk. He is from the Osage village down the river."

"Hello, this is my friend White Snake," says Red Hawk, gesturing toward Wayne Pastor while noticing Big Elk placing his arm around Wy-nu-sa.

"Who is this little brave you embrace and kiss, Wy-nu-sa?" scorns Big Elk, towering over Red Hawk.

"I am sorry, I did not tell you about my first love from earlier this year, Big Elk," informs the Indian maiden, noticing the sadness enveloping Red Hawk. "To be honest, I have more than just affection for both of you."

"This decision, him or me, needs to be made soon," says Big Elk, roughly releasing Wy-nu-sa and walking toward Red Hawk, planting his nose inches from his forehead, "for I am going off to revenge the Whites who have stolen our land."

"I have affections for you both. I don't know how to decide."

Stepping back, Big Elk pokes his right index finger into Red Hawk's chest and spits on his feet. "Let us settle this tonight. Meet me at Hanging Rock when the full moon is bright, and we will resolve it at the top."

That night, as the torch-carrying White Snake and Red Hawk stride their way to the destination that extends slightly over the south bank of the Wabash River, discussion between the two continues.

"You don't have to do this, Red Hawk."

"It is more than just Wy-nu-sa now. He challenged my pride, my dignity as a Miami, and my manhood. I cannot live in disgrace."

"Yes you can. You are my friend, and he is older and bigger than you," pleads White Snake. "Let's just head on down the river right now. Be gone with them."

"You have much to learn about the Indian way, my blood brother. First of all, we will see Big Elk again. You heard him. He is going to Prophetstown for war. Secondly, Wy-nu-sa will be mine. Do not underestimate my fighting skills."

"Yeah, but he is big."

Spotting the torches of Big Elk and Wy-nu-sa, Red Hawk leads White Snake. "There they are. Now listen White Snake, you will stay here with Wy-nu-sa."

Staring through the moonlight and torch-lit air, the four approach and meet each other at the base of the 75-foot Hanging Rock and stare across from each other. The lapping of the river against the bank and a lone wolf howl from the distance cuts the silence.

"Prepare to die, Red Bird," warns an insulting Big Elk.

"I will marry the victor. Remember, I love you both," states Wy-nu-sa, tearing up and turning away.

Up the gravelly limestone trail, the bare-chested Big Elk leads the breech-clothed Red Hawk.

At the uneven, shrubby 15-by-15-foot top, the two step back from each other, holding no weapon exposed in their left hand, but a torch blazing in their right.

"Anytime, you fool," orders Big Elk. "Let's go."

Circling each other and not knowing exactly where the drop-off to the river below is on the north side, Big Elk waves his torch around to distract Red Hawk and disorient him. Sensing a slope, the anxious Red Hawk charges Big Elk to make the first move and prevent himself from accidently falling off.

Dodging Red Hawk, Big Elk shoves his opponent in the back as he goes by, giving a swift kick to Red Hawk's buttocks, hoping his opponent would tumble over the edge and end the fight in quick fashion.

Heading for the blackness of night, Red Hawk desperately reaches for and grabs a shrub that is deeply rooted into the limestone thus preventing a fatal fall. Feeling his legs dangling, he drops his torch and uses his pectoral muscled body strength to pull himself up with two hands.

"I do not hear a yell. I sense, but do not see, my stupid adversary," commentates Big Elk, moving and watching for his counterpart to appear from the edge.

Having obtained safety from a near fall to his death, Red Hawk uses a lower narrow sloped natural ledge to circle around Big Elk. Spotting an opening to attack his adversary, he charges again and catches Big Elk by surprise, wrapping his arms around the warrior's waist. Quickly dropping himself to the hard surface of limestone and pulling Big Elk with him, Red Hawk ignores the pain and uses his body weight momentum and leverage to propel the larger brave over the top of him and thrusts his combatant off the crown of Hanging Rock.

"AHHHH!!! Ahhh!!" SCREAMS Big Elk as he tumbles from the brink, swinging his arms wildly while falling toward the shallow water-covered rocks below.

Red Hawk breaths deeply as he lays face-up staring at the stars, hardly believing it is over. Hearing the scrambling of someone emerging at the summit, he stands to his feet to see Wy-nu-sa extending her torch in search for the victor and realizes that it is Red Hawk. She runs to embrace the man she is destined to marry.

Holding him tightly, she suddenly breaks away from Red Hawk, tosses the torch down, and through sobs utters, "The wrong brave has won. I am sorry, I do not want to marry you, Red Hawk, for it is Big Elk I truly love and cannot live without!"

With that she runs toward the rocky edge and Wy-nu-sa leaps, crying loudly, and plummets to the river below to join her true love.

Red Hawk stoops down to one knee in shocking disbelief. Moments pass as tears roll down his cheeks, and then he hears someone scurrying up the trail to the summit again.

"Are you all right?" calls White Snake, holding his torch out in front of him to seek Red Hawk. "Oh, there you are. I was afraid you went off the other side."

"She did not want me," murmurs Red Hawk.

"I heard a splash," describes White Snake, "and I ran down to the bank to see if it was you, but I could not tell, even with my torch. Then there was another splash near the first body. It was Wy-nu-sa. Still alive, she crawled toward Big Elk and reached out to him, muttering something and then she was lifeless."

Pausing a minute to let the whole event sink in, Red Hawk stands up, wipes the tears and points to the path. "Let's go, let's head down there. Lead the way, White Snake, with your light."

"Dad gum, I'm glad you're still alive, Red Hawk."

"So am I, White Snake, and that term you just used is not Algonquin."

As the two braves descend the steep trail, they are met by ascending villagers who heard the screams of Big Elk and Wy-nu-sa carry across the water through the still of the night.

"Who are you?" asks the first local Miami brave, placing his torch near Red Hawk's and White Snake's faces to identify them. Not waiting for an answer, he orders, "You both come down and follow me. What did you do to our friends?"

"Hold on, now," says White Snake, "I can explain everything."

Reaching the bottom and pulling the pair's arms behind their backs to have them tied, another brave asks, "Why did you shove them off Hanging Rock?"

Two days later, Red Hawk and White Snake sit in the center of a dugout canoe with their feet and hands now tied in front of them. A Miami brave in front and in back paddle the twenty miles of the forest-lined Wabash River toward the Osage village where the Mississinewa River merges with the Wabash.

The canoeist in back raises his dilemma. "This is more complicated now that Wy-nu-sa's mother has died from the heartbreak of her daughter's death. Since we do not have either one of her parents to decide whether they would adopt one of you to take Wy-nus-sa's place, Chief Charley has decided to allow the elders at the Osage village that Big Elk comes from to sort it out. If I were you two, I would not be optimistic."

"Look, we are telling the truth," explains White Snake again.

"Don't you remember my friend Red Hawk visiting the villages last spring with his father, Running Deer, and Wy-nu-sa and him falling in love?"

"It makes no difference now. Red Hawk is alive and Big Elk is dead. Jealousy makes one a fool sometimes," responds the front brave.

"My guess is that it goes before the Seven Pillars," opines the brave at the stern.

"Psst," alerts White Snake to Red Hawk, "those Jesuit priests started praying for us before we left this morning, Red Hawk. I got a little confused with the French spoken, but they were hoping we were not taken before the Pillars."

"Let's hope those prayers help and a miracle takes place, 'cause this place we may be going to, if I remember right, doesn't sound good for us."

Two hours later, the Miami braves canoeing alongside the prisoners as escorts call to familiar faces as the entourage approaches the largest of four local Indian villages, made up mostly of Miami, Potawatomi and French traders.

Landing at the south bank of the Wabash River just past a merging, swift-moving Mississinewa River, the flotilla is greeted by Chief Shepocanah.

"We grieve the loss of one of our best warriors, Big Elk," exclaims Shepocanah. "Our village understands his maiden was also slain by the two Kekiongans you bring to us. The mother of the maiden has died, and the family of Big Elk has moved on, to where we do not know."

Having their feet untied and stepping ashore, Red Hawk and White Snake listen intently to conversations, noting that decision-making elders like Chief Winamac have left for Prophetstown while Chief Squirrel and Chief Palonzwah were away and not expected any day soon. What was most annoying was that Shepocanah, probably from war injuries, couldn't hear very well.

"I do not understand the defense explanation," says the veteran chief of the Indian wars. "You eat now and then take the accused to Seven Pillars for inciteful judgement. I will go partway with you on the way to my village farther up the Mississinewa."

"I don't know who these seven pillars are, Red Hawk," says White Snake, "but I hope they have good judgement."

"The Seven Pillars are a cliff formation, White Snake. The elders that live near there understand the wisdom they will receive from spirits that live in and around the shallow caverns in the cliff. My father told me during our trip down here that those with special powers can pass into the world of the dead and return, perhaps having talked with the deceased to decide what to do, in this case, with us."

Once more, several canoes, including Shepocanah's, escort Red Hawk and White Snake, this time allowing the two to help with paddling against a strong current that was resisting them and through a mist-like fog that has formed as they approach the pillars.

"I see what you mean, Red Hawk," says White Snake. "The Pillars are more like, I don't know, columns supporting the cliff. There is something different here," speaks White Snake nervously, observing and realizing their lives will be affected by the outcome.

Paddling their way to the south bank across the river from the Seven Pillars, the two are taken to a small village 300 feet from the river and into a round wigwam used as a sweat lodge.

The young men are staggered by the heat and darkness upon entering. An unknown sub-chief pouring water on the hot rocks in the center of the room is barely visible. "Now what, Red Hawk?" asks White Snake. "I don't think our guards came in with us."

Red Hawk whispers, "My father told me that in here, everyone will honor the fallen – in this case, those they think we took the lives of – and become purified. We will then be taken to the Pillars for judgement."

Several hours go by with the only interruptions from more heated rocks being brought in, rhythmic drumming and chants of funeral incantation. All involved in the wigwam ritual become delusional in the 100-plus-degree heat and complete darkness until a sorcerous type individual opens the flap and orders all the occupants out.

Taken to the river by warriors and canoed to a platform in front of the Seven Pillars, Red Hawk and White Snake are dropped off and seated while the sorcerer canoes by himself to the Pillars. Through the fog and mist, the sorcerer is seen stepping from his canoe and into the shallow caverns.

"I don't have a good feeling about this, Red Hawk."

"Neither do I, my friend."

On either side of the two blood brothers are special ceremonially decorated warriors wearing horned buffalo skulls on top of their heads and holding large, sharply edged tomahawks, staring at the cliffs and waiting on the orders of judgement.

Minutes go by, which seem like an eternity to Red Hawk and White Snake, when the sorcerer-type elder walks out of the caverns and tosses dust and smoke-like substances into the air. Shouting incomprehensible utterances that only the warriors holding the large tomahawks seem to understand, the boys are told to kneel down.

Joined by four other warriors that tied their canoes to the river stage, the two Kekiongans are lifted up, placed facedown and held flat on their chests with only their heads hanging over the platform edge.

"Goodbye, White Snake," murmurs Red Hawk.

"What is happening, Red Hawk?" sobs his friend.

Curtis, who along with Ostrander is second in command, is seen conversing with Rhea, and the room instantly gets crowded. With the officer's quarters illuminated by four lanterns, stern looks are everywhere.

Mary Wells speaks first, cutting through the greetings. "Captain Rhea, have you heard from my husband? Please tell me you have heard from Fort Dearborn."

"Sorry, Mary. Not a word," replies Rhea, gulping a mugful of hard cider, "but we should see them all any day now."

"I just got word from an Indian who went to Dearborn with William that…" her voice trails off and she slouches into a chair with her daughters' arms easing her down.

Bondie helps Mary finish her statement, "Sorry, Mary, you have to hear this. They're not coming back, Captain. I just talked to my Indian friend Chief Metea of the Potawatomi. Stickney, you hearing this also? Since we haven't got official word yet, there is always hope but, Metea says Fort Wayne is next."

Stickney speaks up, "Captain Rhea we need to get the women and children out of Fort Wayne. Evacuate them to Stephen's brother's place at Fort Piqua. I recommend they leave tomorrow."

Stephen Johnston nervously agrees, "Yes, my … my wi— … wife needs to leave. She is not well. Mary, let's get you and your family out of here, also."

"I'm not going anywhere," states Mary Wells, "but Anne, you and Rebecca and young Mary need to go. William Wayne and I will stay in the fort."

"My wife and children are leaving also," informs Bondie.

Captain Rhea, finally getting a word in, blurts, "Captain Johnny Logan is here from Piqua. Ostrander, go find him. Tell him he's going to be leaving with evacuees in the morning, and I need to see him immediately.

"We haven't heard from Detroit in weeks. Lieutenant Curtis, see if you can't find Private Smith, and we'll send him there."

"Yes, sir."

"We're going to have to move citizens into the fort and get E.J. Carlisle and other scouts out seeing what's going on, Curtis!" concludes Rhea.

Warriors painted for war depart the Osage village located where the Mississinewa River flows into the Wabash River. Most of the Mississinewa Miami who agree with war against the Americans paddle down the Wabash toward a planned siege on Fort Harrison.

Since Red Hawk and White Snake are familiar with Fort Wayne, they are canoeing upstream with Wabash Valley Potawatomi lead by Winamac.

The same evening Mary Wells is receiving sad news from Dearborn, the two Kekionga natives and the Osage village inhabitants have heard that Fort Dearborn has fallen and that U.S. General William Hull of Detroit surrendered 2400 Americans to Tecumseh and the British without firing a shot.

Water lapping and currents flowing into the bow of the Indian canoes brings a greatly desired signal. "Chief Winamac wants everyone to camp here for the night," informs Red Hawk to White Snake in the back of the birch-bark boat.

As the twenty-canoe flotilla rams ashore on the north side of the Wabash River, Miami chiefs already there have camp fires burning.

"If I had known it was you here, I wouldn't have had the braves land," says Winamac. "It has already been discussed, Pechewa, we are going to war."

"You can call me by my English name, Richardville, just like my French and Indian friend Godfroy. Come here, Francis," orders Richardville to his Miami war chief exiting the woods after relieving himself.

"The braves have made up their minds," says the annoyed Winamac. "It is their land they want back. They want the Long Knives out of here! We will have close to a thousand warriors and British soldiers when we all convene at Kekionga. It will be another easy victory."

"Gather your warriors around the fire, Winamac. Enjoy the food my Miami braves have prepared," requests Godfroy. "I want to talk to them about what is at stake."

As the forty warriors secure their canoes and bring their belongings near the fire and set up camp, another individual walks out of the darkest stage of twilight and is exposed by the blazing fires.

Alerted by this stranger dressed in oversized clothing and a long - billed cap followed closely by a wild wolf, the natives grab their weapons.

"Oh, don't worry about my companion," says the white man, speaking in broken Algonquin. "He adopted me rather than I adopted him. Ha!"

Chief Godfroy declares, "Well now, it is no coincidence that we all meet at this place at this particular time. Come in here, Mr. Chapman. Eat with us."

Still leery of the glowing eyes of the carnivore, the Indians don't sit down or relax their arms.

Sensing this, John Chapman turns to the wolf and speaks in English, "It is ok. You wait back there. I'll bring you something later." As the wolf backs away, Chapman ties his worn-down packhorse, carrying bags of apple seeds and other items, next to some Indian ponies. He walks into the firelight and gently greets everyone, creating a natural relaxation that is calming.

"I have not seen you in a while, Mr. Chapman," greets Richardville. "Sit with us. Listen to us. Speak with us."

Not seeing a white man treated this way in several months, Red Hawk and White Snake are amazed by the cordiality he receives and clothing he wears that White Snake is thinking looks like his father's.

"Don't you come in here talking about peace, Chapman," warns Winamac, also acquainted with the white traveler.

"The Great Spirit you worship has put us here for a reason, Winamac," speaks Johnny, reaching out his bowl for some corn meal with the other braves.

Sitting down with his food and speaking with his persuasive voice that commands respect from the Indians to listen, Chapman begins, "Your people have been around here for a few decades, or is it centuries, I'm not sure? You came into this valley seeking a refuge from enemy tribes and Nephilim of long ago. The mound builders that created such huge earthen, intricately formed monuments to something from above that can only be appreciated from up high dominate your land."

"How do you as a white man know this knowledge? How do you receive this?" probes a puzzled Winamac.

"Just like you, my beliefs are one with nature. If one isolates himself and listens in solitude, observes, prays to the creator and studies the Bible that contains God's word, answers can be obtained."

"I understand some of your thoughts," replies Winamac, "but my manitou requires the Americans to be eliminated from our land, forcibly if we must."

"I understand your feelings, but these thoughts are from the evil one that doesn't make you do anything," counters Chapman. "Satan tempts everyone with choices. Then we choose."

"Are you calling my personal manitou demonic?" inquires an indignant Winamac.

"Satan can come to us in many forms to advance his lost cause," says Chapman.

"What do you mean lost cause?"

"Jesus Christ has already defeated death. Satan is trying to prevent as many as he can from accepting Jesus as their savior before the end time comes and a New Jerusalem is created."

"You sound a little like these Jesuits I see along the rivers," informs Winamac as he gets up, waving his hand at Chapman. "This is war, and these braves that follow me know it. It is the only thing the cheating and lying Americans understand."

"The repercussions will be long-lasting, Winamac," says Richardville. "Even if you and Tecumseh are victorious at Kekionga, do you actually think the Americans will stop entering our land?"

"Then we will defeat them again until it stops," argues Winamac.

"Where are your endless sources, Winamac?" chimes in Godfroy. "The Americans are as numerous as the trees. Our people will be punished because of the actions of a warring few."

Richardville stands up to emphasize his point. "We can live among them. Do not fall for this fanatical Tecumseh and his brother. We have been doing good with the whites the last decade. They give us what we need to live among them!"

"Ah, this is all nonsense. We don't need anything from the Americans but our land." Dismissing his warriors to go bed down, Winamac finishes, "My warriors and I move forward to Fort Wayne in the morning!"

A few days later, seven miles north and west of Fort Wayne, scout E.J. Carlisle, remembering his Anthony Wayne days, rides his horse in the woods parallel to a trail – the very trail that led Colonel John Hardin's 180 troops to a defeat to Little Turtle near the Eel River during Harmar's campaign in 1790.

Suddenly, an American wearing a blue uniform of the United States Army staggers by, not noticing E.J.

"Hey, Corporal!" calls Carlisle, startling the soldier.

Stumbling and falling into the brush in a delirious and famished state, the hiding passerby waits for the voice to be identified.

"Get up and out of there, Corporal," orders E.J., "or are you injured?"

"Mister, I'm not sure where I is or where I's going, but I survived the Fort Dearborn massacre and am trying to get to Fort Wayne. Plus, I'm so hungry I could eat a horse."

"Well, let's don't eat Thunder here, cause he's gonna get you and me where you want to go. Now get away from that trail and crawl back in here toward me. I've got some grub for you."

Dismounting his chestnut-colored horse, E.J. grabs the canteen strapped around him and beef jerky from his saddle bag. Assisting the corporal to sit up and receive nourishment, E.J. notices rope around the Corporal's ankles and on his left wrist.

"When you feel up to it, you're gonna have to tell me what happened, Corporal. Corporal Jordan, is it? Is that what I see embroidered on your shirt?"

Taking a bite and then a couple swigs of water, the soldier begins, "Yeah, Jordan's my name. I was with William Wells, rest his soul."

"Wells is gone, you are sure?" questions E.J. "Because the fort hasn't received official word."

"Oh yeah, he's gone all right. I was almost a goner myself as a prisoner destined to be burned at the stake when a Miami acting as a friend of them rascals cut me loose in the middle of the night. He said something about a white guy cutting him loose once when he was a captive."

"Dang, that sounds like Running Deer."

"Yeah, that's him," says Jordan, "he took off too. I don't know if he made it back. Not sure he wants to. The Miami that escorted us were neutral during the battle."

"What happened in the battle?" asks E.J.

Jordan takes another bite and, while chewing, shakes his head and emits, "It only lasted fifteen minutes, but it was god-awful. We had just evacuated the fort, and hundreds of redskins were on us."

"Wait a second," says E.J. "I hear something."

From ten feet off the trail's edge, E.J. softly pats Thunder's side and whispers, "Quiet now, boy."

Barely visible through the brush and trees, the two Americans watch and listen with pounding hearts as Potawatomi dressed in breechcloths run by. Painted for war, the single file of braves head southeasterly in the direction of Fort Wayne.

As the last Indian goes by, Jordan whispers, "I count fifteen."

"You are delirious, Corporal. That was at least twenty-five. Tell me the rest of your story on the way back."

Chapter 10

Late August – Early September 1812 — Fort Wayne/Kekionga Area

Rat-a-tah-tat. Rat-a-tah-tat. Rat-a-tah-tat-ta-tat. Rat-a-tah-tat. Rat-a-tah-tat. Rat-a-tah-tat-ta-tat. Rat-a-tah-tat. Rat-a-ta-tat, ta-tat. Rat-a-tah-tat. Rat-a-ta-tat, ta-tat.

The twin drummers beat out the 5 p.m. roll call muster at Fort Wayne. Falling in line are seventy-one regulars and officers. Fourteen others stay on guard duty, dispersed in either the double-story blockhouses on the corners of the south picket wall, the lookout over the main gate or the large two-story blockhouse on the north picket wall facing the St. Marys River.

The fife musicians join the drummers to play their music and march past the commander's building to escort a hard cider-induced Captain James Rhea to the front of the assembled soldiers.

Rhea raises his hand to silence the band and signals for the list of fort soldiers' names to be read off. As the men respond "Present," Rhea looks over his notes and then takes a gander at the crowded perimeter of the parade ground full of townspeople that chose not to evacuate to Piqua. While waiting to hear the day's news, they listen to the roll call, which finishes with a couple disciplinary comments from Lieutenants Curtis and Ostrander.

Captain Rhea then addresses a normally routine muster.

"D-D-Don't you d-dare fall asleep on guard duty!" begins an obviously anxious and tipsy commander. "With the arriv—, arrival of Corporal Jordan from Fort Dearborn, we now know for sure that William Wells and others there were either taken captive or are now deceased. Let's remove our hats and have a moment... a moment of silence." After a few seconds, Rhea continues.

"Thank you. As you can tell, we are moving the citizenry in from the village. The surrounding forest is infested with Indians."

"Captain, may I interject?" says Lieutenant Ostrander, standing nearby. "We have not heard from Fort Detroit in weeks, and that Private John Smith is currently traveling or returning from there. We understand that Tecumseh has been active at Detroit with the British and has an influence on the natives surrounding us at this location."

"Very g-good, Lieutenant," compliments Captain Rhea. "Indian a-agent Stickney is sick, and perhaps tomorrow, he will give us his assessment. Gates will remain closed. No one is to leave or enter without permission f-f-from me or my lieutenants. Consequences could be f-f-fity lashes. Keep your muskets l-l-loaded, powder dry and bayonets attached.

"Even though we have evacuated m-most of our women and children to Piqua, we still ha-have some in the fort, and I ask that you soldiers treat them with respect."

Looking around at the listening villagers, sutlers and farmers, Rhea's attention turns to them.

"If you have a-a-a musket or rifle, be ready to assist the s-soldiers, or be willing to load extra muskets for them.

"Sleeping quarters w-will be tight. Some of you will be sleeping on horses, I mean floors, or outside. Cattle and h-hogs will remain in the pasture, only closer. You cooks and soldiers be on h-high alert when acquiring for butchering.

"I need to s-see the lieutenants. Any questions, see your officer in charge. Stay on high alert! You may lower the flag, Corporal."

The drummers sound the lowering of the flag, and all attention from the crowd, with hands over hearts, is directed toward the flagpole.

The dismissal drum cadence beats as the military community tend to their business.

"Lieutenant C-Curtis?" requests Rhea.

"Yes, sir."

"Get a messenger off to Fort Harrison that we are currently ok but are surrounded by belligerents and to be aware of hostilities potentially coming their way."

"Ostranderrr, come here!" orders Rhea. Lowering his voice so no one else can hear, Rhea is almost in tears as he says, "To be perfectly honest, I don't think we have a chance, Lieutenant. There are too many Indians out there. I don't want to end up like Wells. Let's go to the headquarters, get a drink, and think this over."

Standing on the officer's quarters porch watching the murmuring soldiers go to their business, E.J. turns to Charlotte. "Dad burn, I wish you had evacuated with Bondie's and Mary Wells' families."

"Don't you swear at me like that, E.J. Don't you remember, you showed me how to shoot when we were with Harmar's army? Besides, if Mary Wells and her son can stay here, so can I."

"Sorry, Charlotte, but you and our kids have never gone through something like this. War is hell, Charlotte. Most of the time, there is no mercy."

"I understand, E.J. I have heard enough of the war stories from you, Uncle Isaac and the poor Captain Wells to know what could happen."

One hundred twenty miles south and east of Fort Wayne, sutlers William Oliver and E.J.'s Uncle Isaac have received their merchandising supplies at Cincinnati and have also received permission to help Brigadier General William Henry Harrison in his efforts to bring the Kentucky militia to Urbana, Ohio, and the headquarters of the Northwest Army.

In the evening at the Harrison campsite along the route from Cincinnati to Urbana, word comes in via messenger from John Johnston of Piqua.

"Urgent message, General," announces an aide-de-camp. "It is from Piqua."

Receiving the envelope and beginning to open it, Harrison glances around at his scouts that include Oliver, Isaac Carlisle and famous pioneer Simon Kenton.

"Carlisle, you say you were kept captive after the Battle of Kekionga around here somewhere? And so were you, Mr. Kenton?"

"Well, I got nabbed out of Kentucky by the Injuns and brought up this way," mentions Kenton casually. "Ran the gauntlet a couple times before escaping."

Pausing to let Simon Kenton's brief story sink in, Uncle Isaac emits, "I was a few minutes from being burned alive General, before my nephew by the act of God saved me."

"Seems I've heard a few stories like that before," says Harrison, looking down at and then reading the message to himself. After finishing, Harrison rubs his chin, looks up and asks, "Oliver, where are you from? Fort Wayne, did you say?"

"Yes, sir. I run a little store in the village," answers the 25-year-old.

"Seems they have evacuated women and children from there to Piqua," informs Harrison.

"No kidding, sir?" speaks up Uncle Isaac. "We both knew Indians were forming around the fort but thought they were just heading for Piqua for a council meeting. We have kin in Fort Wayne, General."

"Yes, figured you did, Carlisle. Kenton, I want you to make your way up to Fort Malden and Fort Detroit. Check on what the British and Tecumseh are up to.

"Oliver and Carlisle, you two take your packhorses to Piqua and a message for John Johnston to send you and Captain Johnny Logan, if he is still around there, to Fort Wayne to see what the situation is.

"Logan is a good Shawnee scout also known as Spemica Lawba. He knows his stuff, and he has some friends. Leave tonight, as soon as you are repacked, for Piqua and then to Fort Wayne with Logan. Head back to Piqua with Fort Wayne's condition as soon as possible. My army may have to divert to Kekionga!" orders the future president of the United States.

Paddling up the Wabash River past the regretful Hanging Rock and busy Forks of the Wabash, the Potawatomi and Miami warriors, including Red Hawk and White Snake, make their way to the often used portage campground twelve miles from Kekionga.

Being the last camp before seeing Fort Wayne again, the boys' pent-up feelings surface.

"Red Hawk? Psst, Red Hawk?" murmurs White Snake, rolling over in his bedding near his friend.

"Yes, what is it?" answers Red Hawk, not quite asleep yet.

"Feels weird traveling back home," replies White Snake. "It doesn't feel like home, though."

"I know what you mean, White Snake. I grew up in Kekionga, but I really started getting used to living in the Osage village," says Red Hawk. "I think I am over Wy-nu-sa and the Hanging Rock incident. Besides, there are a couple young Indian maidens I like there, also."

"I am glad for you. Although my time with Shepocanah and Maconaquah was good, I didn't feel like I fit in."

"You just have to give it time, White Snake."

"Well, there is more to it. I've been thinking about how to handle this upcoming siege."

"We knew this could possibly happen when we left our fathers a year ago, remember?" says Red Hawk. "As far as I'm concerned, they are Americans. We are now committed to Winamac and Tecumseh. King George of England is now our father."

"Dad burn, Red Hawk, I get all that. But, but, I can't watch or participate in the killing of my family or yours at Fort Wayne or anywhere."

"I can tell you what to do, but you must know it in your heart, White Snake. Do what you have to do," replies Red Hawk. "Know though, that if you leave our tribe, you will always be my blood brother, but I must wash my hands of you."

Later that night, White Snake gathers his belongings and sneaks away from a smoldering campfire and sleeping braves toward the portage trail that takes him to the St. Marys River. By the time daylight has broken, he has traveled the twelve miles by foot to the put-in place near Kekionga.

From the way he is dressed, the Potawatomi and Miami tribesmen that are spread out in the forest surrounding Fort Wayne do not suspect his defection.

In the woods a half mile from his old abandoned farmhouse, White Snake is noticed.

"Where you go?" speaks a Potawatomi of the north in the Algonquin language. "You know we must stay out of sight of the fort until given the signal?"

Not quite understanding the dialect, White Snake smiles and nods but keeps going.

"You not understand? Who are you?" follows the persistent brave.

This, White Snake fortunately picks up on and stops to answer, "I am White Snake of the Miami. I come from Mississinewa. What news or instruction can you give me?"

"The fort is surrounded by many braves. We are waiting for the British. They and Tecumseh should be bringing many soldiers and warriors from Canada with large cannons," reports the grinning informer. "I wish to add to my collection," brags the Indian, pointing to the American scalps around his waist and attached to his Brown Bessie British musket.

"I will not go much closer," agrees White Snake deceptively.

"Wait, where are your Miami brothers?"

"They will be coming. I am an advanced scout," lies White Snake, taking off running.

"No, you wait!" exclaims the warrior, running back to get awakening friends to help him chase the deserter down.

Sprinting through the woods and then onto a trail that White Snake remembers leads to his former farmhouse home, he breaks into the open pasture and dashes full speed to his large homestead cabin.

"Man, I should have done this at night," announces a panting White Snake to himself.

Ducking out of sight and inside the vacant living quarters, he finds his clothes in his former sleeping area that are still where he left them a year ago. Hearing the yipping and howling of advancing warriors in the distance, he hurriedly rips off his breechcloths and washes the war paint with a towel and convenient bucket of water the best he can.

Hopping around to quickly fit into his buckskin pants and then a linsey-woolsey shirt, he snatches his dad's coonskin cap off of a hook. Just as he places it on his head, he hears the Potawatomi getting louder outside the rail fencing that surrounds the cabin.

Wayne Pastor grabs his Indian rifle, tomahawk and scalping knife that his Miami friends had given him at Deaf Man's Village and scurries out the cabin door.

Alarmingly, the first Indian leading the pursuers rounds the corner of the cabin just as Wayne Pastor is exiting. With one swift move, Wayne Pastor takes his knife by the blade, stops, and hurls it, striking the tomahawk-carrying warrior in the chest, dropping him two strides later.

Sensing more urgency, he takes on the quarter-mile run to the fort entrance by hurdling over the top rail of the front yard fence and landing just as he hears musket fire from the Potawatomi behind him. Musket balls whiz by, except for a stray one that nicks his earlobe.

Feeling the blood dripping from his ear to his neck, he zig-zag runs, hoping to avoid a direct hit and the lead he has on his chasers is enough to reach the fort gate safely.

Breathing heavily, the former Indian gets within shouting distance of the southwest blockhouse, waves his hat, and gasps a shout at the fort lookouts, "Don't shoot, it's me, Wayne Pastor! Don't shoot!"

Bam! Bam!

They shoot anyway, knocking down a swift Indian that was about to catch Wayne Pastor from behind resulting in a halt to the Indian pursuit. Grabbing their fallen brother, the slower Indians just arriving drag him back out of range.

Avoiding being struck by either the Indians desperately trying to stop him or by the Americans by mistake, Wayne Pastor arrives at an opening south gate.

After a day of elated welcoming Wayne Pastor home and hearing some of his harrowing stories, concerns grow at the fort as three men are preparing to ride to Piqua for help.

"Now listen, Mr. Johnston. Stephen, is it?" asks Wayne Pastor, still draped by his parents, Charlotte and E.J.

"Yes, Stephen Johnston. I've been the clerk around here for Mr. Stickney. We have to go. It's almost 10 p.m., and my two friends and I want to get to Piqua by late morning."

"It's just, you better ride hard to get through," says Wayne Pastor. "From what I saw and was told by a Potawatomi, the noose around Fort Wayne is getting tighter. There are hundreds of Indians out there and more expected with the British any day."

"Look kid, you're gonna have to speak clearer Algonquin. I can understand some of what you're saying, but dag nabbit, slow down," replies an anxious Johnston.

"Yeah, yeah, sorry," responds Wayne Pastor, and then he repeats everything in English.

Indian agent Benjamin Stickney limps around Johnston's horse to get a closer look at his clerk. "Surely there is a better way to go than Wayne Trace."

"It's the fastest way from here to there," answers the clerk.

"Yeah, but they're gonna be watching it!" says his friend and boss.

"I gotta see how my wife is, Benjamin. You know that. Her health has been failing," replies Stephen.

"Here, Stephen, take my sword," offers Antoine Bondie, handing it up to him. "You may need it."

"Thanks, Mr. Bondie, I have just the sheath here for that," reacts Stephen as he slides it in.

"Maybe I should go with them," suggests Wayne Pastor.

"Oh, now dad burn, son," says E.J., "you just got here. Let's get you settled in first."

"Yes, Wayne Pastor," says his mother, "perhaps fewer the better, and you already had your close call for the day. How's your ear, by the way?" says Charlotte reaching up to touch it.

"Aww mom, It's all right," says Wayne Pastor pulling away.

"Yep, and we ain't waitin' for you to saddle up and everything," says Peter Oliver. "Me and my partner here are ready to go, and the horses we are on are the fastest in the fort. Especially Stephen's. We'll tell his brother what's going on. He'll send relief."

"Open the gates!" shouts Oliver. "We'll see you all when we see you!"

The guards on duty, using lanterns to identify everything, begin to push the main gate open to the pitch black of night. Giving their mares a side kick, the three riders wave a farewell at the group and then disappear into the darkness with the sound of pounding hoofs following the well-worn trail to the southeast.

As Stephen's fast stallion gallops ahead of the other two, sporadic campfires a mile away from the fort are seen in the forest on either side of them. Riding low in their saddles and leaning forward with their head on the side of their horse's heads and grasping the mane with one hand, they make progress down the trail and grow confident in making it through until several torch-bearing warriors step out, halting Stephen's horse and grabbing the reins.

The store clerk draws his sword and swings wildly, striking one native and severing his arm drawing the ire of the others. A spear thrust to Johnston's side by a warrior penetrates through his body. With blood gushing everywhere by the spear being pulled out, the wound causes him to fall off his horse and into the arms of waiting braves, who stab him repeatedly and lift his scalp.

Stephen's two companions several yards behind pull up. "Did you see that, partner?" asks Peter Oliver.

"It's hard to tell, but I think they got Johnston!"

"That's what I saw, and we're next if we don't get outta here! Come on. We can't help him," orders Oliver, as they turn their horses around and kick them into high gear back to Fort Wayne at full speed.

Two days later, Chief White Raccoon rides his undersized pony up to the closed main gate of Fort Wayne, leading a packhorse with the covered body of Stephen Johnston draped over it.

In Algonquin, he yells to the overhead guard post, "I have come for my reward from Mr. Bondie. I have the person he requests."

The gate slowly opens, and regulars on duty walk up to retrieve the packhorse.

Lowering his rifle at the soldiers, "No, you pay reward first of twenty dollars, then take body only," demands White Raccoon. "Also, Chief Winamac desires a white flag so he may meet and speak with the fort commander."

While the chief waits, Antoine Bondie walks out the gate with the money and asks, "Why did this happen? He had done nothing but help your people at the factory."

"Young warriors, Mr. Bondie. They are hard to control."

Pulling the blanket back to identify the corpse, Indian agent Stickney, who has joined Bondie, is horrified. "My God, Chief. I can hardly identify him."

Johnston's body is carried in the fort by guards, and a white garment is attached to a short pole and presented to the Indian.

"You will hear from Chief Winamac soon," informs White Raccoon.

"The flag is good for one day only," advises Stickney. "Captain Rhea expects Winamac before the next sunrise."

White Raccoon smirks and rides away.

The next day, preparing for a possible attack, wood planks are placed along the inner picket wall on top of barrels for forces to stand on to shoot over the picket fence.

Along the permanent banquette, facing the west, soldiers shout down to an officer, "Sergeant, we have Indians coming with the white flag!"

The sergeant gives a whistle to the southwest blockhouse, and personnel inside wave back that they acknowledge the flag leading a hundred braves approaching on foot.

"They're not coming to the south gate, Sergeant. They are herding some cattle and hogs to take away."

"Do we have permission to shoot, sir?" asks a soldier, aiming his musket along with others over the picket wall.

"They have a white flag. Hold up, men," orders the sergeant, jumping up on the platform to get a view while a messenger scampers to the commander's building to get orders.

"Do not fire, do not fire!" commands the quick-paced, advancing Lieutenant Curtis, who had heard the alarm and already received the order.

"But Lieutenant, we can't let them get away with this!" yells a private.

"This is embarrassing," complains another.

"Those Indians are making fools of us," grumbles a corporal.

"Just follow orders, men. I'm assuming the captain has his reasons," explains Curtis as he steps up on a banquette to have a look himself.

After a night at the fort of Americans grousing about losing food on the hoof and stolen garden produce the previous day, they are forced to watch Chief Winamac ride up to the main gate with four other chiefs, one of which holds the white flag.

"I ought to plug them right there," says a blockhouse guard, aiming his Springfield musket at the flag-carrying chief.

"Don't do it, Private," warns his corporal. "Captain would prolly hang ya for disobeying ordas."

"Might be," says the private, pausing to eject a spit of his tobacco, "worth it."

"I wish to speak with the fort commander!" requests Winamac, wearing a breechcloth, leggings, silver earrings, moccasins and a deerskin shirt. With the spear he holds containing attached American scalps, his war paint glimmers while he studies the Fort Wayne walls and blockhouses.

Five minutes go by until the gate opens. The five chiefs dismount their ponies and are led in prudently by Curtis and Ostrander.

Chapter 11

Stepping through the entrance of the south gate, Winamac, Five Medals, the familiar Metea and two other chiefs representing the nearby Miami tribe drop their weapons and are taken to Captain James Rhea's headquarters. On the long walk to the building at the northeast corner of the fort, they pass by a nervous, silent crowd of onlookers. Children that were not evacuated to Piqua hide behind the skirt or pant legs of their parents, who are standing on the porches that overlook the parade grounds. Regulars at attention dressed neatly in uniform sport their bayonet-glistening muskets.

Greeting the chiefs on the front porch of his headquarters, Captain James Rhea smiles broadly as he escorts his wife, Polly, out of the building and away from the door that the chiefs will soon enter. Interpreters Benjamin Stickney and Antoine Bondie wait in the captain's office for the meeting to begin.

The chiefs file in and take a seat offered to them across a desk from Rhea's chair.

Captain Rhea enters, sets down glasses for them and requests as he pours, "allow me to get you chiefs some wine to drink with me?"

Winamac and his advisers unabashedly lift the glasses and down their drinks.

Captain Rhea then goes to the point. "So what do you chiefs want, peace or war?"

Winamac glares at Rhea and answers, "I just want to remind or inform you that Detroit has surrendered, Forts Mackinac and Dearborn have fallen into our hands, and you will be next!"

"Here, have some more wine," mollifies Rhea, pouring more wine and then responding. "Listen, Winamac, I will fight for you. I will die by your side. You must save me!"

Rhea pulls out a half-dollar and hands it to Winamac. "Come back in the morning for breakfast," invites Rhea, now begging. "You must save me. I love you." The interpreters can't believe what they are interpreting. For that matter, neither can the chiefs standing up to leave and visibly disturbed by what is being witnessed. "No return for breakfast!" shouts a sub-chief as the five file out the door and head to the main gate to walk back to their camp.

Captain Rhea watches the chiefs leave from the porch and then walks back in to tear into his aides inexorably. "That was the worst case of interpreting I have ever witnessed! Those chiefs left here about as confident-looking as I have ever seen Indians. We need to send a messenger to Governor Return Meigs of Ohio as soon as possible that we need assistance immediately. I don't care if the messenger gets killed on the way. We'll send another! Dad burnit!

"Gentlemen! I think we should consider surrendering the fort," says an emotional, irrational, drunken Rhea, taking a long gulp of wine and slamming the glass down on his oak desk, startling everyone and causing Polly Rhea to peek in the doorway to see if everyone is ok.

That night, red- and black-marked William Oliver and scout Captain Johnny Logan, a full-blood Shawnee raised by Americans, approach the Kekionga area riding cautiously northwest from Piqua with Logan's Shawnee friend, Bright Horn.

Oliver carries word from Indian agent John Johnston that Harrison and the American military are on the way and that Fort Wayne should hold on if they can. The three realize the tricky part will be getting the message inside the fort and then getting back to Harrison safely with the temperament of Fort Wayne.

Encountering pro-Winamac warriors on the outskirts of the offensive perimeter was the first line of business.

"You bringing help from Piqua?'" asks a torch-bearing Potawatomi, without warning, stepping out of the darkness and startling the trio, with a spear pointed at Captain Johnny.

"No, no, we are here to help defeat the Americans," soft sells Bright Horn to the suspicious but trusting Indian. "Let us go through."

"You go to Frenchtown first and ask for Metea. He will let you know the situation, and then go see Chief Winamac and be updated on tomorrow's strategy."

"That will be ok with us," says Johnny Logan, helping the war-painted Oliver so he doesn't have to speak his lousy Algonquin.

Riding their horses north to the Maumee River a mile and a half east of Fort Wayne, they dismount and tie their horses to branches. The plan to slip in and out of the fort begins with a walk along the Maumee riverbank west to survey the situation. Carrying their hunting rifles, they manage to get to the northeast corner of the fort unseen, but there is no one on the wall to signal to that they need in the north river back gate. Unable to hail anyone, they return to their horses and ride the same path that they walked.

In an attempt to get to the main gate, they ride up the riverbank to the west side of the fort and startle two Indians rounding the northwest corner. The Indians, thinking it is the lead force of a rumored Harrison army arriving, take off running toward the Indian meeting grounds to the west howling, "They are here! The Americans are here!"

In the darkness, disregarding the hightailing Indians, William Oliver and his two cohorts make their way to the southwest blockhouse and shout, "Let us in! Let us in, dad burnit!" Recognizing Oliver's voice, those inside open the main gate with great relief.

Oliver dismounts and greets friendly faces. "Yeah, it's me, Oliver, dad burnit! Listen, it may take a while, but Harrison is on the way!

"Captain Johnny, I can't leave these folks," informs Oliver scrawling a note on some parchment. "You and Bright Horn, take this written letter informing Harrison that Fort Wayne is intact. I would suggest you partners go back the same way we came and give a yell once you've broken through the Indians."

At once, the compliant companions take a couple swigs of whiskey offered to them, walk their horses to the north river gate and mount their rides.

"You boys can make it! Ride like hell, fellas! Nothin' can stop ya!" come the encouraging words cascading from the soldiers on the now occupied picket wall and in the north blockhouse. Taking a deep breath and giving a nod, the two Shawnee burst out the gate to ride along the stony and rocky shoreline of the Maumee, easterly this time, but they have to pick up the pace when they see torch-carrying Potawatomi riding their ponies hard after them from the west and closing the gap.

"How did they know we were heading out?" asks Bright Horn to Captain Johnny in Algonquin.

"They're watching the gates! Let's go!"

"AHYA! YA AYA! YA! AHYA! YIP YIP YIP!" cry the posse warriors, angry that messengers are getting through. On a couple of John Johnston's best steeds, Captain Johnny and Bright Horn are at top stride when they are intercepted by three Miami warriors exposed by a full moon breaking through heavy clouds. The warriors leap from the 15-foot-high south riverbank, intent on ruining the messengers' mission. Two land on the horses' back quarters but are gashed off by the wild tomahawk swings of the riders propelling them into the rocky shallow Maumee with a splash thud.

The third of the three braves lands and grabs the bridle of Johnny Logan's mount but is met with a tomahawk blow to his neck, spraying blood across the horse's right flank.

Giving a snap to their leather reins and a side kick to spur their horses back to full gallop, the two pull away from the pony posse and give a loud yell to let the garrison know they were getting through. "Yee! HAA! Yee Ha Ha Haaa!"

"YEAH!" cheer the men on the eastern picket wall in response, relieved there is a good chance that word will soon reach Harrison.

Later that night at the main Indian camp three quarters of a mile southwest of the garrison, Potawatomi Chiefs Five Medals, Winamac and Metea meet with Miami leaders representing a total of 500 warriors.

The native chiefs finish eating a roasted hog they had taken from the Americans and are now ready to strategize.

"Tomorrow, we take all of our warriors with us to the main gate," speaks Winamac. "Under the cover of the white flag, we will ask to speak with Captain Rhea again. They will ask us to drop our weapons outside the gate, but I want you to conceal one under your garments. The signal to pull them out and kill as many Americans as you can will be when I say, 'I am a man.' The one who is closest to the gate will open it and let our braves in. No one shall be spared. Eliminate all the Americans! Easy enough?"

"I think that will work, Winamac," Five Medals agrees.

The rest grin and nod affirmatively.

"Let us all meet midmorning here, and we will walk to the fort together. Spread the word, but no war dance tonight. Americans must suspect nothing but peace talks when we approach.

"That drunken fool Rhea must believe nothing but agreeable terms when we walk in with smiles. Bring tobacco, Metea. Each bring their pipe," instructs a grimacing Winamac to the chiefs.

The next morning at the appointed time, several hundred braves congregate at the camp, anticipating lifting scalps at the fort and ending the siege. Red Hawk paces around wondering what he is going to do when and if he encounters his best friend, Wayne Pastor, or longtime family friend and his father's scouting partner, E.J. Carlisle.

Finally the chiefs, led by Winamac, step in front of the warriors representing different Potawatomi and Miami clans and begin the walk toward the fortress that has a fifteen-star American flag flapping gently in the breeze above it.

Carrying a flag of truce, Chief Winamac stops several paces from the main gate and hollers at the lookout above, "We wish to meet with the American commander!" Close to five hundred warriors stand behind him. Winamac observes the gate cracking open and Indian agent Stickney limping to meet him and stating, "You cannot all come in!" Stickney then rattles off Winamac and twelve other Indians that he knows by name to enter the fort to parley. "The rest must stay out here."

The thirteen Indians walk to the fort entrance but are halted. "Hold it right there, chiefs!" exclaims Stickney. "Leave your weapons at the gate. All of them!" The chiefs hesitate because of their concealed weapons and because they immediately notice a military unit on the parade grounds standing at attention in full arms.

Antoine Bondie, assisting Stickney, attempts to calm the alarmed Winamac. "Don't worry, Chief; with all the warriors you brought with you, we just want to feel safe ourselves. Sorry to inform you, you will not meet with Captain Rhea. He is not feeling well. We will talk in Mr. Stickney's quarters. Come right this way."

Passing by the edgy patrons of the fort, a portion of the Indian delegation enters Stickney's makeshift office, leaving the others outside. Taking a seat, Metea pulls out his tobacco.

Stickney, knowing it is customary at Indian parleys before negotiations begin, draws out his pipe and tobacco. Smiling to keep things calm, he offers tobacco all around.

With a lantern lighting up the single-windowed room, Winamac is comforted when he sees Five Medals peering through to watch the proceedings take place.

Smoking until all the tobacco is used up. Stickney breaks the small talk. "What's the deal, Chief, with using the white flag to steal our hogs and cattle, and the killing of my clerk Stephen Johnston?" Feeling the tension rising, Stickney finishes, "You have soiled the white flag!"

Winamac rises and sternly looks at Stickney with displeasure. As his war-painted facial features shine from the minimal sunlight entering the window, he responds, "My Potawatomi did not kill your clerk. It was young warriors that were unable to be controlled causing the mischief!"

"We have heard that before," says Stickney. "Is your leadership too weak to contain them?"

Interpreters, struggling to stay up, pause when Winamac shouts, "Enough with your insults! Does my father wish to have war?"

Winamac then exposes his concealed hunting knife. "I am a man!" The phrase signals the chaos to begin.

Bondie, seeing the seriousness of Winamac, intervenes by standing up also and drawing his knife, yelling, "I am a man, also!"

Winamac, thinking the other chiefs in his presence would follow the plan and pull out their concealed weapons, looks out the window and sees a pensive Five Medals shaking his head, signaling to call it off.

Winamac slams his knife down point first into Stickney's oak desk and states, "then we will have to settle this the hard way!" He twists his knife out of the desk, defiantly snatches his pipe and strides out the doorway toward the gate. Watched closely by the soldiers standing at the ready and those in the blockhouses observing, the chiefs file behind the obviously disturbed, wide-eyed Winamac.

Gathering their weapons at the fort gate, the disappointed Winamac walks back to the camp contemplating the next move and wondering when the British will be arriving with Tecumseh and the artillery to blast the walls of Fort Wayne down.

Awakening from his alcohol-induced nap, Captain James Rhea steps out onto his headquarters porch holding and waving a partially empty whiskey bottle, yelling, "Stickney! Bondie! Ostrander! Lieutenant Curtis! Get over here! You, Private, standing over there! Straighten out your hat! At least look like a soldier!" rants the random-thinking Rhea, taking another long swallow from his bottle. As the officers walk toward Rhea, the captain takes another swig and pulls out his Long Knife sword and this time waving it around.

"Don't you men ever meet with those redskins again without me! Do you understand? Why, I ought to hang you all from the gate right now to send a message to everyone in here and out there that I mean business! From what I saw through the gate, the Indians have too many warriors! There is no way we can hold them off!"

Taking another swig and waving his bottle around, Rhea's expletive-laced rant continues. "Why, with Tecumseh and the dad burned British coming with their cannons they captured at Fort Dearborn, it is just a matter of time!"

"Captain!" says Stickney while Bondie and the lieutenants gesture to calm him down. "We can stop them! We can do it, Captain! The largest artillery piece they had at Dearborn was a three-pounder. No one surrenders to a three-pounder! You gotta stop drinking and listen to us!"

"You guys don't know anything. Tuck your shirttail in and look like an officer," demands the slurring Rhea, performing a teetering about-face maneuver. Rhea then staggers back into his headquarters and falls onto a bed into a fetal position. Shaking nervously with fear of an Indian attack, his imaginative thoughts are compounded by the description of Dearborn's massacre by survivor Corporal Walter Jordan.

"Rhea!" yells Stickney through the doorway. "You are done! Lieutenant Ostrander and Curtis are taking over the command until Harrison gets here. Anyone who thinks this command should surrender to an imaginary three-pounder should be shot."

"No, no! Don't shoot my husband!" screams Polly Rhea. "James, James, snap out of it!"

"Aw, Polly! I am sorry I got you into this mess," says Rhea, rolling over to grab his whiskey bottle.

That night at the main Indian camp, Red Hawk and four Miami friends finish their stew of beef chunks and vegetables harvested from a Fort Wayne raid.

"This meal reminds me, brothers. The Americans usually leave the fort early in the morning to retrieve their produce from the garden they have outside the fort. Let's make our way to their root house before sunrise and ambush them in the morning," suggests Red Hawk in Algonquin. "We may not get any scalps immediately, but the psychological damage and lack of food may push them toward giving up the fort sooner rather than later."

"I like that idea. Let's not tell the chiefs our plan and sneak down there," suggests a young warrior, smiling anxiously for the action.

"Yes, I'll wake you guys when it is time to go," says Red Hawk. "Sleep with your musket."

The next morning, Red Hawk wakes the braves to virtually start a siege battle that both sides are delaying until help arrives from either Malden, Canada, or Piqua, Ohio.

In the pitch darkness just before the break of dawn, the young warriors make their way silently following Red Hawk, who knows the terrain around Fort Wayne imminently. Crouching their way to the building next to the garden, they set up under cover, laying in wait.

While the Indians are biding their time near the root house, reveille is drummed out to awaken the Americans and call them to the parade grounds for the orders of the day.

Rat-tat-tat. Rat-tat-tat. Rat-tat-at-tat. Rat-tat-at-tat. Rat-a-tah-tat.

Rousing soldiers grumble, "I'll tell ya what they can do with those drum sticks if I have to wake up one more morning to them guys marching around here beating their confounded drums!"

Hearing the men complaining coming out of their barracks, Wayne Pastor and his dad converse, "they better think about what they are upset about," says E.J.

"I agree, Dad. If those Indians have their way today, that will be the last time they may hear American drums."

"That's right, son. Like your great-Uncle Isaac, they may end up hearing the drum beat of warriors while waiting to be burned at the stake."

"Let's hope this fort is man enough to withstand that kind of result," says Wayne Pastor.

"Elmer James?" calls Charlotte from inside their temporary living quarters tending the younger children. "You and Wayne Pastor out there?"

"Yes, Dear," responds E.J.

"Those boys tending to the vegetables back from the root house yet?"

BAM, B-bam, Bam! Shots ring out from outside the fort.

"That could be them now, Charlotte, and it may not be good! Come on, Wayne Pastor, let's see what's going on," says E.J.

As they break for the main gate, they hear voices from above, "We got two men down, E.J., near the garden and root house! Indians ambushed them!" comes the information from the blockhouse on the southwest corner.

"Cover us, Sergeant, and you guys on the wall!" yells E.J., remembering Fort Recovery. "We'll go bring them in!"

"E.J.! Don't be a fool! Wait till we sort the problem out! It's too dangerous out there!" responds a corporal on the wall banquette.

Not heeding the advice, E.J. and Wayne Pastor run along the outside of the fort wall to gather at least one of the downed soldiers to drag him back to the gate.

In bushes near the root house, Red Hawk comments to the warrior on his right. "I knew that would bring more Americans outside. "Load up, brothers!"

Taking aim, Red Hawk lowers his sights on the two whites running to help the wounded soldiers and notices the familiar running gaits of E.J. and Wayne Pastor. Shots from the wall sail by Red Hawk and his war party, harmlessly striking trees, bushes and the walls of the root house. Red Hawk, having Wayne Pastor clearly in his sights, slowly begins to squeeze for a fatal shot on his friend when he feels a musket ball graze one of the feathers on his head, startling him into realizing what he may be doing. "Cease-fire!" he yells in Algonquin as he watches E.J. and Wayne Pastor carry one of the injured soldier's body to the main south gate entrance.

Red Hawk's nearest companion sprints out to the other American laying injured and quickly slices off the top layer of head and scalp, ignoring the scream of the still-conscious injured soldier. He then quickly zig-zags his way back to the cover of the root house, luckily avoiding the musket balls being fired from the western picket wall of Fort Wayne.

"Yaa-yaa! Hee-yaa!" crows the Miami, waving the scalp of the lifeless American at the regulars who are peering over the wall frantically trying to reload their muskets to get a shot at the arrogant brave.

Dying in the arms of E.J. and Wayne Pastor, the soldier who was pulled to safety says, in his last breath, "Thanks. At least they didn't get my hair."

"Those dad burned rascals," says E.J. "We gotta stop them!"

"You dang fools!" calls Charlotte, running up. "Are you two crazies ok?"

A constant firing of weapons back and forth from the walls directed at the Indians and the Indians harmlessly striking the wall in return stirs E.J. and Wayne Pastor back to the reality of the situation.

"Yeah, we're ok," answers E.J. "Charlotte, get the kids out here to help reload muskets. Hurry now, go get them out here. They've been taught how to do it!"

Lieutenant Ostrander runs up to E.J. and Wayne Pastor. "Man, I just heard what you guys did! That was very heroic!"

"Thanks, Lieutenant, but be prepared. Just like at Fort Recovery back in '94, the Indians will either try to chop their way in at a weak spot in the wall, scale the walls with ladders, or burn us out!"

"Oh yeah, E.J. I remember your stories. Cease-fire, men, and load up!" commands Ostrander. "Let's make them think we are out of ammo and maybe they'll come out in the open to attack!"

The trick doesn't work as the Indians stay hidden.

"Two cannons, sir, on the hill where the old fort used to be!" calls a lookout from the main gate overlook.

Chief Winamac, on his pony and carrying the oft used white flag, rides down the hill toward the front gate followed by hundreds of warriors and calls for Stickney.

"Yeah? What do you want? A bloody nose?" bellows a voice from the southeast blockhouse.

"This is your last chance! We are going to blast your walls down," yells Winamac, "and storm in!"

"Those don't look like real cannons, and you don't know how to fire them anyway," counters Lieutenant Curtis, taking control of the situation by speaking for Stickney.

"I say bring it on, Winamac! What do you guys say!?" yells Curtis at the men on the walls and in the blockhouses.

"Yeah, bring it on, you varmints!" yell the cheering regulars and those inside the fort ready to hand reloaded muskets up to the riflemen on the banquette.

The Native Americans react by screaming back in an attempt to drown out the American noise.

YAYAYA! Ah-YAAA! YIPP-YAAH!

Both sides scream the best they can to intimidate the other, as if the loudest will be victorious when this siege is over.

"HA!" laughs Ostrander after the yelling has subsided. "Through my spyglass, those look like hollow logs, Chief!" hollers Ostrander from the gatehouse standing next to Curtis.

As Winamac retreats his braves up the hill and toward his camp to reorganize, Ostrander climbs down off the platform and sidles up to E.J.

"What do you think they will do next, Carlisle?" asks the lieutenant.

"Be ready for any of those things I told you about earlier, sir. Definitely have those howitzers in the blockhouses loaded and ready."

Chapter 12

September 6 – 12, 1812 — Fort Wayne at Kekionga

As a constant early evening barrage of musket balls rocket back and forth between the combatants, warriors cluster under cover behind cottonwood and oak trees twenty yards from the northeast corner of the picket enclosure, as if a weakness had been detected. With the likeness of shooting stars, arrows with pouches of gunpowder attached to the tip are set aflame and shot by the Indians over the east pickets toward the western picket wall and the barracks just a few feet from it.

Serving as a distraction, the western wall fire is small compared to the torches the hustling warriors carry up to the northeast corner. Dry branches are thrown down first, and then torches are tossed on them, creating a blaze that lights up the Indians, making them easy targets for the Americans in the large north blockhouse.

Rolling the 8-inch howitzer cannon to the window facing east, a fuse is lit.

BLAM!

Projectiles nick and directly hit the braves, forcing loud winces of pain as the Indians duck around to the east side pickets to avoid the blockhouse howitzer.

The fire and warriors on the northeast corner are clearly noticed by Americans manning the southeast blockhouse. Although 130 feet away, the soldiers frantically aim their howitzer out the north porthole and fire along the wall.

Blam!

The wider scattering projectiles maim and deal a death blow to those natives wanting to enter the fort at that corner. Carrying and assisting their wounded brothers, the braves head back into the forest for cover.

"Buckets! We need buckets of water over here!" yells Ostrander, heading to the well located near the western wall next to the brick ammunition and weapon magazine building. Village sutlers that have been watching their businesses west of the fort go up in flames join women and children carrying anything that holds water to toss on the fires.

Flaming arrows flying over the walls find their mark on the dry wooden shingles atop the 1800 Colonel Hunt fort structures.

William Oliver, taking charge of the civilians inside the fort, organizes a bucket brigade line of panic-stricken ladies and children that lead to men climbing a ladder to the roof of the commander's burning headquarters.

Horses attached to the tie line raise up and stir with fright from the turmoil.

Meanwhile, at the southwesterly wall, Indians are scaling ladders to breach the barrier. Steady American musket shots from the southwest blockhouse knock Indians off of the ladders and to the ground and on top of warriors below that are waiting to ascend.

One Potawatomi makes it over and drops to the banquette next to Wayne Pastor who is reloading. The Indian's momentum takes him past Wayne Pastor and to the ground landing next to E.J. Carlisle, who is directing the civilians reloading weapons.

"Look out, dad!" warns Wayne Pastor too late.

Struggling to ward off the native, E.J. finds himself on his back with the warrior bringing a knife toward his chest. Pushing back with his left hand around the right wrist containing the knife of the warrior, his right hand struggles to hold off the Indian's left hand fingernails digging into his face. E.J. feels himself drawing weaker as the warrior uses his weight to press the knife down.

"E.J., E.J.!" yells Charlotte nearby helping to reload muskets. "Get off my husband, dad burnit!" screams E.J.'s wife as she runs toward the native.

Holding an old 10 pound French Charleville musket by the gun barrel, Charlotte swings to strike the warrior on the side of the head with the buttstock.

With everything happening so fast, Wayne Pastor drops to the ground to help. "Get the Indian's arms, mom!" commands Wayne Pastor who snatches a rope. "Bring them around his back!"

The dazed warrior lying face down does not resist and allows himself to be tied by Wayne Pastor just as E.J. wipes the blood off his right cheek and rises to his feet catching his breath.

"Thanks everyone, but I had him all the way," says a smiling and winking E.J. scanning for more Indians coming over the top of the wall.

BLAM!

The three family members jump as the final discouragement to this attack is a howitzer blast from the southwest blockhouse toward the ladder scalers. The resulting metal fragments rake Indians off their ladders, killing two immediately. The warriors retreat behind the outbuildings, council house and Indian agent's factory for protection.

All that night, a steady barrage of musket shots, designed to keep the Americans awake and on edge, are projected on the inhabitants of the fort. Under the cover of darkness and their Brown Bessie musket ball fire, warriors sneak up to the picket walls to carry away wounded, dying and dead brothers.

"Look, Captain Johnny, I know they need help," says Harrison at Piqua, Ohio. "I can read the letter! If you want to ride ahead and tell them we are waiting on flints, be my guest. We are worthless without that triggering flint spark that will ignite the priming! Hopefully, they will arrive tomorrow and we will be moving out to beat the British and Tecumseh to Fort Wayne!"

"Where is Simon Kenton or that John Smith guy that were sent down the Maumee?" inquires a nervously pacing Logan.

"Scouts of some sort should be back with information on that front soon," answers Harrison.

Back at Kekionga, on the western border of the deceased William Wells's property, Running Deer and his son Red Hawk sit together amongst a cluster of sycamore trees with an unobstructed view of flames sporadically flaring up on buildings in Fort Wayne. As they watch, the two listen to Americans yelling for water to save the buildings and to drench those that are still dry.

Off in the distance, undiscouraged warriors are heard chanting as they dance at the main camp clockwise around pounding war drums, charging themselves up for perhaps a final, victorious attack the next day.

Very little is said between the father and son, so when John Chapman bursts through some branches with his wolf, it is more than startling.

"Take it easy, fellas, it is just me and wolf here," comforts Johnny, noticing the fires in the distance.

"What you watch reminds me of Deuteronomy 20:4, 'for the Lord your God is the one who goes with you, to fight for you against your enemies, to save you,' Bible prophecy. Are you saved, brothers?" asks Chapman.

"Don't call me your brother, Mr. Appleseed, or whoever you are. You are white, I am Indian," says Red Hawk.

"It is best that you listen to his wisdom, Red Hawk," speaks his father.

"Your father is right, Red Hawk," says Chapman. "God is my father, and He is yours. He knows no colors of people. His written word is in the Bible. Are you proud of what has happened to the American fort?"

"Well, Chapman, it is not all the way down, but yes, my people have done good," says Red Hawk confidently.

"As it is said in Micah 7:8, 'Do not gloat over me, my enemy! Though I have fallen, I will rise. Though I sit in the darkness, the Lord will be my light.'"

"You can see that fort ablaze is finished, Chapman. They will be ours tomorrow," predicts Red Hawk. "So don't give me your Biblical truths."

"Let's be respectful, Red Hawk," says Running Deer.

"You don't understand, Father," responds Red Hawk. "I could have killed Wayne Pastor or Mr. Carlisle today, but I did not. Isn't that one of your God's commandments, Mr. Chapman?"

"He is our God, young brave, and what about the one or ones you did kill? War is hell, Red hawk. From what I have read in the Bible, 'Nations that went to battle without the favor of God rarely win the war.'"

"Just go back to your spreading of apple seeds," says Red Hawk, "you have no influence here at Kekionga."

"I suppose you do, young warrior? I spread apple seeds much like I pray to spread love, peace and joy to the inhabitants of earth. This wolf doesn't see hate, he sees food to eat and the need to defend himself, and he attacks for that purpose. What do you see, Red Hawk, when you see whites roaming where your people once dominated? Is it love or hatred? Has hatred gotten you anywhere or just temporarily made you feel better?"

"I am not listening to you, Chapman," falsely states Red Hawk.

"A lot to think about, young warrior. Hopefully you will survive tomorrow's battle to spread the love of Jesus, the only one who can save you from the lake of fire," finishes Chapman, spreading his clothing and a blanket in order to sleep in comfort.

The next morning at Fort Wayne, smoke still smolders as men repair damage with new timber that had been laying around for repairs for weeks.

"Man, it could have been worse, Lieutenant," says Stickney. "We have only lost two men so far, and that was at the beginning of the siege. It could have been windy, and the flames could have been spread everywhere."

"We need to prepare for another onslaught, Stickney," advises Lieutenant Curtis. "I'm surprised they haven't attacked already. Let's continue wetting down ev'rything that is flammable and filling up every vessel we have with water. Another group can load up the extra muskets and rifles we have."

"You fools, we need to offer a peaceful surrender," advises the still drunken Captain Rhea staggering out from his headquarters. "There is no way this fort can withstand another attack! Throw up a white flag!"

"Captain Rhea, your conduct will be reported to Harrison. Get back in that building! You are no longer in charge here!" demands William Oliver, coming along and overhearing Rhea's rants. "Stickney, Curtis," says Oliver, "I back everything you are doing. Harrison told me personally he will be coming to help us,"

Chief Winamac rises next to his campfire to greet Miami and Potawatomi scouts riding in on Wayne Trace.

"How far is Harrison from Fort Wayne?"

"We spotted them at a place the Americans call Shane's Crossing at the St. Marys River, repairing wagons. Harrison is bringing troops as numerous as the trees, Chief Winamac. I'd say they are two days away."

"Chief Metea!" calls out Winamac to the local Potawatomi leader. "You know that trail well. I need for you to slow Harrison down. Set up some ambushes. The warriors here will push to take this fort today one way or another. The British are supposed to arrive with hundreds of reinforcements. Be gone, Metea! Bring us good news about stopping Harrison!"

Harrison's 2200-man army moves northwest much in the Anthony Wayne style for fear of a surprise attack. On the road, Colonel Samuel Wells and a rifle regiment lead Harrison's army, followed by the music of the band. Protecting the right wing is Colonel John Allen and Kentucky volunteers. On the left are Colonel William Lewis's regiment of Kentuckians supported by Colonel John Scott's. The wagons and packhorses are in the middle of the road, with horsemen from Ohio watching the right flank and Major Johnson leading mounted riflemen guarding the left flank.

A mile and a half ahead of the main force are spies, including veteran scouts Captain Johnny, Chief Bright Horn and old friends Uncle Isaac and E.J. Carlisle's best American friend, Bobby Fulton. Bobby, now married with family near Fort Greeneville, Ohio, has heard that his old buddy E.J. at Fort Wayne was in trouble and volunteered to help. Since the Western Pennsylvanian Fulton goes back to the General Harmar and Mad Anthony Wayne days, he is familiar with the trail and terrain.

"We are a good day's travel to the fort yet," says Bobby, "and this is prime ambushing area. It's getting dark. I say we tell Harrison to camp at this location and use the redoubts and temporary defenses already here."

"Sounds good, Bobby," says Uncle Isaac. "I'll ride back to tell him."

"Keep your gun cocked, Ike. I've been hearing some suspicious sounds. Captain Johnny, Bright Horn and I will clear the land around the redoubts that are already built."

"Ok, Bobby. You guys be careful also, I've seen some shadowy movement, and I don't think it's just turkey buzzards."

"Whoo, Whoo, whoo!"

What are assumed to be owl sounds are heard by the trio, creating a nervous atmosphere while prepping the camp.

Ike brings an agreeable Harrison, a half mile back, forward but not without alarms and quick dismounts and drawing of weapons by Sam Wells's riflemen. "This may not be a good time, but I've been meaning to ask you, Ike," hesitates the navy blue-jacketed, high red-and-white-collared militiaman Colonel Wells, fast-walk leading his horse, "has there been any word of my daughter Rebekah and her husband, Captain Heald?"

"Sorry, Colonel. Last I heard was that after the Fort Dearborn massacre, they had been taken captive and were seen in a boat heading to northern Lake Michigan. Perhaps a trade for their return can be worked out," offers a sanguine Uncle Isaac.

Back at Fort Wayne, after a day of constant musket fire back and forth and a refusal by the Americans to evacuate the fort, darkness sees fire arrows ignited again and flung at the walls and roofs with little effect on the now water-soaked material.

"What is that large fire to the southeast?" asks Lieutenant Ostrander. "That's in the direction of Harrison's approach. Could that be his army in a battle with the Indians and British?"

"Or a lure for us to come out and see if it is?" counters Lieutenant Curtis. "Whatever it is, let's don't allow the Indians to trick us and just stay put until we see Harrison, himself."

Pitched tents of Harrison's camp and his manned redoubts are observed by the blackened and eerie-looking Chief Metea as he creeps around to get a good look at what his Indian force is up against. While Harrison is relieving himself at the edge of the camp, he notices Metea and pulls out his 1805 .58-caliber flintlock pistol. He slowly aims and fires at a shadowy figure behind a honey locust tree thirty yards away.

BAM!

Metea drops his hunting rifle and grabs his wounded right elbow. Deciding to sprint away from the danger, he realizes thirty yards later that he could never live down the dishonor of returning to his braves without his rifle.

Sneaking back and wincing in pain, he avoids guards of Harrison combing the area looking for traces of blood to track him down. Finding his rifle, Metea pulls his scalping knife, preparing for close-quarter combat. A pursuer of Metea is startled by a fellow guard searching for the chief and fires blindly, striking a comrade in the chest and wounding him mortally.

"Surgeon! I need a surgeon over here!" yells the apologetic rifleman. "I'm sorry, Mac! I'm sorry, Mac! Surgeon!" The sound of the gunfire and the guard alerts other guards to call for help and to warn others not to shoot them.

Metea sees the confusion as a time to make a run for it and meet up with his fellow braves to tell of the information he has obtained during his close call.

The next day, E.J. and Charlotte have their arms around each other, gazing sadly over the western wall into the late afternoon sun.

Observing their farmhouse and barn burning, tears stream down their faces.

Crops are being destroyed throughout the countryside. Earlier, the council house, root house and Indian agent Stickney's factory had been ravaged and torched. The tears of sadness and the toil they had placed in living at Fort Wayne causes them to ignore the musket balls flying overhead and off the pickets. Also being ignored are the Indians running past the eastern wall, away from the trail Harrison would bring in to encounter the siege and end it.

At the large blockhouse overlooking the St. Marys River, Wayne Pastor shares an open window with Captain Rhea, who now feels well enough to shoot at a frantic Indian retreat crossing the river. In the distance, Wayne Pastor and Rhea watch William and Mary Wells's farm being consumed by fire and livestock shot.

BAM!

"There goes another one, Wayne Pastor. Shoot him!" says Rhea, hurriedly reloading his musket.

Getting a bead on the Indian, Wayne Pastor realizes he has a clear shot at Red Hawk.

"Shoot him! Shoot him! Before he gets away, you idiot!" yells an insolent Rhea.

Moving his musket to another target, he sights Running Deer high-stepping across the shallow Maumee ford toward the orchard of Kekionga.

"Dag nabbit! Give me that gun if you ain't gonna shoot!" demands the commander, grabbing the weapon and accidently discharging it harmlessly into the sky.

BAM!

Exasperated, Rhea utters, "How could you turn down a shot like that!? My gosh, boy, you have a long way to go to be anything like your daddy!"

Standing up to walk away from the window, Wayne Pastor doesn't hear the captain ranting any longer. He no longer cares. He silently walks down the stairs of the blockhouse and exits the door to the cheers of the Fort Wayne defenders greeting the relief of William Henry Harrison's army riding in to end the siege.

Chapter 13

"Isn't this great, Wayne Pastor?" says his ash- and tear-smeared mother, waving her hand at the mostly Kentucky militia being greeted by Lieutenants Ostrander and Curtis, who are giving directions on where to set up their camp and place the steers and hogs that were brought along for food.

"Yeah, it's great, Mom," responds Wayne Pastor, wondering what's next.

"What can I do for you folks?" asks a black-robed Reverend Matthew Wallace, Harrison's army chaplain, as he sidles up.

"I see you carry the good book, Mister," inquires Wayne Pastor

"Oh yes, son. Wouldn't be caught without it," answers Reverend Wallace.

"That's good. You know I was named after the last pastor we had here at Kekionga."

"Oh, is that right?" inquires the reverend curiously.

"Unfortunately, he died a few days before I was born. Injuns got him, right down there in the river," says Wayne Pastor, pointing toward the shallow, murky Maumee as if they could see through the charred picket wall of Fort Wayne. "Hope you have better luck."

"Oh, ha-ha, so do I," laughs the reverend, looking around and drawing his half-cocked pistol out of his robe.

"Oh now, Reverend, don't you worry," says Charlotte. "Wayne Pastor was born in the back of a wagon when the fort was dedicated or close to being finished. I don't remember exactly, but we sure are glad to have you."

"Is that so? And thank you. It's good to be out of that black swamp and off that wilderness trail!"

"Pastor, you are a sight for sore eyes," chimes in E.J., walking up. "We have been needing something like you around here for some time.

I mean, we have this character that shows up once in a while, but he's more of an apple orchard spreader.

Uncle Isaac trots in on his brown horse, dismounts and is followed shortly by a horse-backed Bobby Fulton, gazing about at the damaged fort with his rifle across his lap at the ready.

"Holy cow!" exclaims E.J. "Look who still has his scalp? You guys must have ducked really fast! Ha!" laughs all three, slapping each other on the back, shaking hands and feeling thrilled to be reacquainted again.

"Reverend, we want you to meet our friends," says Charlotte, pulling Reverend Wallace by the robe toward E.J.

"Holy crap! Sorry, Reverend. Is that Smitty riding in, fellas?" asks E.J., looking past the pastor.

"By golly, I think that is," remarks Uncle Ike.

"Smitty! Over here!" yells Bobby, waving.

Riding to the group, Private John Smith is happy to see them but appears distracted. "Good to see you all again, but I gotta report to Harrison, pronto, if you knows what I mean!"

"Yeah, yeah," answers Bobby. "But I haven't seen him yet. What's going on?"

Dismounting his horse, Smith shakes everyone's hands and blurts, "Simon Kenton and I saw a huge amount of British and natives coming up the Maumee with artillery. They have a ways to go, but they is a comin'!"

Pulling himself back onto his horse, he says, "Sorry, I gotta leave so quick, but I have'ta find Harrison and then go jump in that river and take a bath. I stink!"

Everyone laughs and waves as he rides off toward the lively music of a fife and drum band leading Harrison into the fort.

Chapter 14

"Oh geez, there's Josh and Jake backing their wagon up to pick up the grave remains," says Stan.

"Let's get over there and harass them a little bit about Mrs. Harrington," says Nyle, half grinning.

As the two walk toward the gravesite, they encounter a policeman.

"Not you guys again?" says Deputy Sheriff Donnie Bork, walking to relieve a fellow officer watching over the excavation. "Dad burn, didn't I just see you guys last spring rounding up some skulls down the street?"

"Yep," says Nyle. "I don't think Mrs. Harrington ever did get over that surprise found in her basement."

"What do we have here?" asks Bork.

"More pioneer remains, officer," informs Stan.

"Man, this city is full of this type of thing," says the officer.

"Listen, Officer Bork," says Stan. "We have to tell you about some stranger walking through earlier today and then disappearing."

"Oh no, here we go again, Josh," says Jake, standing in the grave and overhearing the vociferous Stan approaching.

"Ok, what's the description?" asks Bork, pulling out his pen and pad to take notes.

"Looked like he was wearing an old military uniform. He was wondering what happened to the fort."

"The old fort that sat here was over 100 years ago," apprises Bork.

"He had the name Ostrander on his coat. Lieutenant insignia maybe? Couldn't quite make it out," says Stan. "Walked toward the graves from where we were working and disappeared."

"All right! That's all I need to hear! We are out of here, Jake," says Josh as he and his partner grab the stretcher to carry the last of the remains to their horse-drawn wagon to reinter at the old cemetery near Broadway and Jefferson streets.

"You think we're making this up?" exclaims Stan. "Well, we're not."

"It's getting too weird again," says Jake, walking back to the grave site to backfill the holes.

"Hey, when you guys gonna get a truck?" asks Nyle.

"When we get a job like that coal company employment of yours, Nyle. Ha!" says a laughing Jake, now settling onto the wagon bench seat next to his brother.

"Probably easier work, too. Ha! You guys take care!" yells Josh, swatting the horses with a snap of the reins. The jerk of the team pulling forward throws his brother off-balance, flipping him back over the seat and into the bone remains.

"Dag nabbit!" Jake grumbles, hearing laughter from Nyle and Stan while climbing back onto his seat.

"Take Superior Street, Josh," requests Jake, rubbing his head. "I wanna see if anyone's along the St. Marys there to fish with tonight."

"I don't know what you're gonna catch. Maybe an old boot again?" jokes Josh.

"Hey, who is that walking down the bank to the river?" asks Jake. "Looks like he is wearing that old uniform the guys were describing. What's he doin' wading across the river for? I'm gonna yell at him. What was his name? Ostrander, was it?"

"Yeah, Ostrander," answers Josh.

"Hey, Ostrander!" yells Jake. "OSTRANDER! Lieutenant!"

"Geez, you have to yell so loud right in my ear? I think the whole city heard ya."

The stranger plodding through the ankle- to shin-deep water of the St. Marys ford finally stops. He turns around, salutes sharply and about-faces, then continues to walk uneasily and disappears before he reaches the other side.

"Did you see that, Josh?" asks Jake.

"I want to say no, but I can't."

Jake jumps off the moving wagon and trots to the riverbank, calling into the dimly lit evening. "Ostrander! Ostrander! Are you all right?"

Scurrying back to the wagon, Jake climbs aboard and asks his brother, "You think he is drowning in a sink hole?"

"I know of no sinkholes along there, Jake. Let's go back and report it to Bork."

"What do you think happened to him, Josh?" asks Jake.

"I don't know, but I just got a cold shiver."

EPILOGUE

1812 – 1813 — Indiana Territory/War of 1812

During the month of September in 1812, to prevent further Indian attacks, General William Henry Harrison ordered Indian villages, crops and supplies destroyed within a fifty-mile radius of Fort Wayne. Specific locations included the Forks of the Wabash near Huntington, Indiana, and Five Medals Village on the Elkhart River near Goshen, Indiana. All Indian villages along the Eel River were wiped out, including one east of Columbia City that put up some resistance to the American forces but to no avail. Finally, Little Turtle's village about twenty miles northwest of Fort Wayne was eliminated, but his home at the time before his death, built by the U.S. government, was left standing.

A siege at Fort Harrison at the same time that Fort Wayne was under assault resulted in another future president of the United States having an involvement in the War of 1812. Captain Zachary Taylor helped lead the defense against a force of 600 Miami, Potawatomi, Kickapoo and Winnebago Indians. Later in his life, he became the fifteenth president of the United States.

Harrison, by order of President James Madison and the U.S. Defense Department, turned his command over to Brigadier General James Winchester at Fort Wayne. Winchester proceeded to follow the Anthony Wayne Trail carved out in 1794 to Fort Defiance to thwart the advancement of Major Adam Muir and Matthew Elliot's combined Indian-British army advancing on Fort Wayne.

In order to quicken their retreat from Winchester's army, the British, much to the chagrin of the Indian force, rolled their artillery pieces into the Maumee River.

As a side note, the author of this book, during his research, discovered that a 3-pound brass cannon and chain was snagged during gravel dredging in the Maumee River for a U.S. Highway 24 project east of New Haven, Indiana, in the 1920s. The author mistakenly thought the cannon, located in a 90-degree bend in the river just northeast of the Whispering Creek Golf Course, was perhaps from the Muir retreat.

The brass cannon was reportedly secretly pulled out of the river by workers during the night, loaded onto a horse-drawn wagon and driven to a local barn. Unfortunately, it was cut into pieces to be sold as scrap and was never seen again.

Cannons allegedly from Muir's retreat have subsequently been snagged or seen in the Maumee River near Defiance, Ohio.

Another theory on the New Haven cannon is that supplies at times from Fort Wayne to Fort Defiance and Fort Winchester were transported by flatboats or barges, one of which may have broken a chain during a sharp left turn because of a fast, high water current. This may have resulted in a cargo shift, spilling the artillery piece into the river.

Muir's coalition was driven back north by Winchester's forces, and a Fort Winchester was built along the Auglaize River six hundred feet south of the 1794 Fort Defiance built by Anthony Wayne.

Captain James Rhea was arrested by Harrison, but charges would be dropped if he resigned effective December 31, 1812. Rhea and his family left Fort Wayne a few days after the siege was over, after he had signed the agreement.

American forces, encouraged by Harrison later that fall, attacked Indian villages along the Mississinewa River, which led to the Battle of the Mississinewa on December 17 and 18, 1812.

In a push to return Fort Detroit to American possession, Kentucky militia, advancing down the Maumee River in their summer clothing under the direction of General Winchester, encountered a late fall/early winter super-cold, heavy snow event six miles northeast of Fort Winchester. Exposure to the cold and frostbite, as well as the inability for supplies to reach them before starvation, led to scores of brave volunteer Kentucky militiamen dying. Witnesses of Camp No. 3 nicknamed it "Fort Starvation."

September 12, 1812 — Fort Wayne at Kekionga

October 1915 — Old Fort Park/Fort Wayne, Indiana

Markers and graves can be found today at Independence State Park east of Defiance, Ohio. When the Wabash and Erie Canal was dug through the area a few decades later, many remains of these soldiers were found and had to be moved to a site nearby in order for the canal to go through.

Lieutenant Philip Ostrander was replaced as temporary commander of Fort Wayne by a 20-year-old nephew of George Rogers Clark, a Major George Croghan. Croghan subsequently was reassigned to Fort Defiance after being replaced at Fort Wayne by Captain Hugh Moore.

Ostrander died mysteriously in late April of 1813 in isolated confinement for, while in an alcoholic state, disobediently discharging his weapon at ducks flying overhead. Buried somewhere near the first or second American Fort Wayne, his grave site has never been located.

Maconaquah, also known by her American name of Frances Slocum, was reacquainted with her white family of Pennsylvania in 1837. Despite urging from her natural brother to move back to Pennsylvania, she lived out her life with her Native American family near Peru, Indiana.

Colonel John Allen from Kentucky, who was one of the first to sign on with Harrison died during the War of 1812 at the Battle of River Raisin in Michigan. Allen counties in Indiana, Ohio and Kentucky are named in his honor.

Shawnee Chief Tecumseh met his demise at the Battle of the Thames near Chatham, Canada, on October 5, 1813. The Indians, after seeing their leader killed, surrendered to Harrison at Fort Detroit and were allowed to peaceably return home.

In August of 1814, during the War of 1812, the British burned the president's mansion in Washington D.C. The fire was extinguished by hurricane-force rain that also spawned tornadoes, which ripped through a retreating British army, killing at least two.

A portrait painting of Chief Little Turtle hanging in the White House was destroyed during the fire.

The Star-Spangled Banner was written by Francis Scott Key during a British bombardment of Fort McHenry near Baltimore, Maryland, on September 14, 1814.

Within three years of the siege at Fort Wayne, a third American Fort Wayne was constructed by fort commander Major John Whistler. He replaced parts of the 1800 fort but kept the same site. Whistler had also helped construct the original 1794 fort and the second one commanded by Colonel Thomas Hunt.

William Henry Harrison went on to be elected the ninth president of the United States in 1841, but he died thirty-one days into his first term of pneumonia, typhoid or high fever. He became the first president to die in office.

Harrison's death in office spawned the twenty-year curse theory that Tecumseh and his brother "The Prophet" allegedly placed on the U.S. presidency. Beginning with Harrison, every twenty years, an elected president would die in office. The curse stood until Ronald Reagan broke it in 1980.

Tenskwatawa, also known as "The Prophet," had wounded himself in the right eye, costing him his vision at a young age. He tried to rally the forces Tecumseh had gathered but failed and lived out his life in Michigan, Indiana, Ohio and Canada, traveling from place to place.

After the siege, Fort Wayne had a few Native American flare-ups, but mostly, it was peaceful around Kekionga.

John Chapman, also known as "Johnny Appleseed," continued to accumulate wealth through land acquisitions and died allegedly a wealthy man on the Archer farm on the north side of Fort Wayne, Indiana.

As a side note, John Chapman, according to documents, bought land in 1840 east of New Haven, Indiana, on the same day as Mitch

Harper's great-great-grandfather, William Harper. Mitch became one of the youngest Indiana State Representatives ever elected in 1978 and served until 1990.

Sources say that John Chapman spent a portion of the last days of his life visiting and spinning tales with friend William Harper at William's log cabin home. Chapman's death came from pneumonia perhaps triggered by a long walk the next day to the Archer family home located where the Canterbury Green apartment complex now is in Fort Wayne, Indiana. He died on March 18, 1845.

Captain Johnny Logan, also known by his Indian name Spemica Lawba, was killed by the enemy while scouting for the United States during the War of 1812. He is buried on the old fort grounds at Defiance, Ohio. A full-blooded Shawnee, he died fighting against the leadership of a full-blooded Shawnee, Tecumseh.

Accreditation and Further Reading

Bodurtha, Arthur Lawrence - "Miami County Indiana, The Story of Francis Slocum." *Indiana Genealogy Trails*, 2020. genealogytrails.com/ind/miami/frances-slocum.html.

Castaldi, Tom - "Indian Agents a Factor in Early Fort Wayne." History Center Notes and Queries, from *Fort Wayne Monthly* "Along the Heritage Trail with Tom Castaldi," No. 139, August 2016. historycenterfw.blogspot.com/2016/12/indian-agents-factor-in-early-fort-wayne.html.

Eggleston, Edward and Lillie Eggleston Seelye - *Famous American Indians, Tecumseh and the Shawnee Prophet*. New York: Dodd, Mead & Company, 1878.

Gale, Neil, Ph.D. - "An In-depth Analysis of the Fort Dearborn Massacre on August 15, 1812," *Digital Research Library of Illinois History Journal*, 2018. www.drloihjournal.blogspot.com/2018/07/an-in-depth-analysis-of-the-battle-of-fort-dearborn.html.

Griswold, Bert J. - *Fort Wayne, Gateway of the West, 1802–1813. Garrison Orderly Books, Indian Agency Account Book*. Indiana Historical Collections, Vol. XV, Indianapolis, IN: Historical Bureau of the Indiana Library and Historical Department, 1927.

Griswold, Bert J. - *The Pictorial History of Fort Wayne, Indiana*. Chicago, IL: Robert O. Law Company, 1917.

Heath, William - *William Wells and the Struggle for the Old Northwest*. Norman, OK: University of Oklahoma Press, 2015.

Hickman, Kennedy - *War of 1812: Siege of Fort Wayne*. ThoughtCo, Updated 6 Nov. 2019. www.thoughtco.com/siege-of-fort-wayne-2361364.

Historic American Indian Tribes of Ohio - Rocky River City Schools, June 2019.   -
www.rrcs.org/Downloads/Ohios%20historic%20Indians%2038%20pag es.pdf.

"John Chapman, Also Known as 'Johnny Appleseed - Early American Pioneer Nurseryman and Swedenbordgian Missionary." The *Swedenborgian Church of North America*, 2020.
swedenborg.org/famous-swedenborgians/john-chapman/.

Kettler, Sara. - "7 Facts About Johnny Appleseed." *Biography,* 21 June 2019.
www.biography.com/news/johnny-appleseed-story-facts.

Lewis, Orrin and Laura Redish - "Native American Facts for Kids: Miami Tribe." *Native Languages of the Americas*, 2015.
www.bigorrin.org/miami_kids.htm.

Lossing, Benson J. - *The Pictorial Field-Book of the War of 1812*. New York, NY: Harper and Brothers, 1868.

Myaamia Community Blog – *Aacimotaaiiyankwi* –
www.aacimotaatiiyankwi.org, 2020.

Poinsatte, Charles - *Outpost in the Wilderness: Fort Wayne, 1706-1828*. Fort Wayne Historical Society, Fort Wayne, IN: Allen County, 1976.

Raynor, Keith - "The Battle of the Mississinewa 1812." *The War of 1812* www.warof1812.ca/mississa.htm. Accessed 2020.

"Seven Pillars of the Mississinewa" - *Orangebean*, 5 Dec. 2019
orangebeanindiana.com/2019/12/05/seven-pillars-of-the-mississinewa

Sherman, Walter J. - "Old Fort Industry and the Conflicting Historical Accounts," *The Historical Society of Northwestern Ohio*, Bulletin No. 3, July 1930.

Slocum, Charles Elihu - "Fort Miami and Fort Industry, Other Forts in and Near the Maumee River Basin." *Ohio American History & Genealogy Project*, Defiance, OH: 1903. ohahgp.genealogyvillage.com/Resources/forts-miami-and-fort-industry.html.

Slocum, Charles Elihu - *History of the Maumee River Basin*, Indianapolis, IN: Bowen & Slocum, 1905.

"The Miami Nation of Indiana" - *Miami Nation of Indians of Indiana* www.miamiindians.org. Accessed 2020.

"War Paint - Meaning of colors of War Paint, Body Paint or Face Painting" - *Native Indian Tribes*, site seen limited, 2018. www.warpaths2peacepipes.com/native-american-culture/war-paint.htm.

Winkler, John F. - *Tippecanoe 1811: The Prophet's Battle*. New York, NY: Osprey Publishing, 2015.

Story characters in the approximate order of appearance in the Kekionga three-book series

F – Fictional
nf – Non-Fictional

The Bones of Kekionga

Nyle (F) – Fort Wayne resident construction worker, coal deliverer, driver

Stan (F) – Fort Wayne resident construction worker, coal deliverer

Bob Gavin (nf) – Fort Wayne resident amateur historian

E.J. Carlisle (F) – Pennsylvania militia volunteer, pioneer frontiersman, scout, dragoon member, farmer, guide

Mike Fink (nf) – Flatboat navigator, former scout, ranger

Uncle Isaac Carlisle, Uncle Ike, Ike (F) – Uncle of E.J., frontiersman, farmer, volunteer militiaman, cavalryman from Pennsylvania, scout, merchant, guide

Ben Conrad (F) – Young militiaman volunteer from Pennsylvania

Bobby Fulton (F) – Young militiaman volunteer from Pennsylvania, scout, dragoon member, frontiersman, guide

Charlotte (F) – Young pioneer girl from Pennsylvania with her family. Girlfriend then wife of E.J. Carlisle, mother of Wayne Pastor

Major James McMillin (nf) – Kentucky militia officer

Major James Paul (nf) – Pennsylvania militia officer

Daniel Boone (nf) – Frontiersman, owner of Boone's Tavern, scout, guide

Simon Kenton (nf) – Frontiersman, scout, guide

Governor and General Arthur St. Clair (nf) – Governor of the United States Northwest Territory, General of the Northwest Army

General Josiah Harmar (nf) – Revolutionary war veteran, commanded the first American Regiment in the old Northwest Territory

Nathan Boone (nf) – son of Daniel Boone

Henry Hay (nf) – British trader at Kekionga

Chief Little Turtle (nf) – Mishikinakwa, Miami Indian war chief

Antoine Lasselle (nf) – French trader and trapper

Running Deer (F) – Miami Indian brave and warrior

Morning Bird (F) – Miami maiden, girlfriend and then wife of Running Deer, mother of Red Hawk

Tecumseh (nf) – Shawnee brave, warrior and war chief

Richardville (nf) – "Pechewa," last civil chief of the Miami Indians, son of Tah Cum Wah and nephew of Little Turtle

John Kinzie (nf) – Fur trader from Quebec, resident at Kekionga and later Chicago

Chief LeGris (nf) – Miami Indian leader during the Northwest Indian War

Mr. Barthelmis (nf) – Pioneer resident of Kekionga

Mr. and Mrs. Adamher (nf) – Pioneer residents of Kekionga

Father Louis Payet (nf) – Resident priest at Kekionga from Montreal

Long Snake (F) – Young Miami brave

Chief Blue Jacket (nf) – Shawnee Indian war chief

Daniel Williams (nf) – Frontiersman, scout and guide

Private John Smith (nf) – Soldier in the U.S. Army

Major John Whistler (nf) – Revolutionary War veteran and member of the U.S. Army during the Northwest Indian War

Major David Ziegler (nf) – Officer in the first American Regiment under Harmar

Mrs. Thacker (F) – Camp follower and cook with the first American Regiment

Major then Colonel John Hamtramck (nf) – Served in the Revolutionary War with Washington as well as with General Anthony Wayne during the Indian War, first commander at Fort Wayne

George Washington (nf) – Served as commander of American forces in the Revolutionary War, first president of the United States

Nathaniel Greene (nf) – Renowned American general in the Revolutionary War

Johnny Dee (F) – Composite guide, scout, frontiersman for Harmar

Degadaga (F) – Composite Iroquois Indian scout, guide for Harmar

Pastor (F) – Harmar and Wayne's composite army chaplain

Colonel John Hardin (nf) – Rancher, farmer, Kentucky militia leader and later peace delegate leader

Colonel James Trotter (nf) – Kentucky militia commander

Tah Cum Wah (nf) – Sister of Little Turtle, mother of Jean Baptiste Richardville, co-operator of the portage from St. Marys River to Little Wabash River

Chiksika (nf) – Brother of Shawnee warrior Tecumseh

William Wells (nf) – Frontiersman, Miami warrior, guide, scout, Indian agent, husband of Little Turtle's daughter Sweet Breeze, Chief Little Turtle's friend, husband of Mary Wells

Lieutenant Colonel Christopher Truby (nf) – Pennsylvania militia leader with Harmar

Captain John Armstrong (nf) – Member of U.S. Army with Harmar

Captain Asa Hartshorne (nf) - Officer under General Harmar and later Anthony Wayne

Black Snake, Apokonit, Carrot Top (nf) – William Wells's Indian names

Major Horatio Hall (nf) – Officer in the first American regiment under Harmar

Major James Fontaine (nf) – Cavalry commander of Harmar's first U.S. Army regiment

Major John Wyllys (nf) – Military officer with General Harmar during Indian War

Major James Ormsby (nf) – Militia officer with General Harmar

Lieutenant Ebenezer Denny (nf) - Military officer with General Harmar and Governor/General St. Clair, future first mayor of Pittsburgh

Sheriff Reichelderfer (nf) – Allen County (Indiana) Sheriff

Sheriff Clausemeier (nf) – Former Allen County (Indiana) Sheriff

Josh (F) – Undertaker

Jake (F) – Undertaker

The March to Kekionga

Mrs. Harrington (nf) – Early 1900s Fort Wayne resident

Robert McClellan (nf) – Scout, ranger, extraordinary athlete, guide, supply packhorse driver

Mr. Sutherland (nf) – Supply packhorse driver

Phillip (F) – Charlotte's younger brother

Simon Girty (nf) – British Indian agent

Buckongahelas (nf) – Delaware Indian chief

Black Hoof (nf) – Head civil chief of the Shawnee

Alexander McKee (nf) – British Indian agent

General 'Mad' Anthony Wayne (nf) – Revolutionary war hero commanding forces against the British, he was later named commander of the United States Army of the Northwest and served in the Northwest Territory. He created a militia called The Legion which was the forerunner of what they call The Old Guard today.

Major Alexander Trueman (nf) – Officer in the U.S. military during the Revolutionary War and the Northwest Indian War, leader of a peace delegation

Sweet Breeze (nf) – Wife of William Wells and daughter of Little Turtle

Secretary of War Henry Knox (nf) – Revolutionary War veteran, served in President Washington's cabinet

General Rufus Putnam (nf) – Revolutionary War general, organizer of the Ohio Company and the settling of the Northwest Territory in Ohio

Sam Wells (nf) – Brother of William Wells, leader of Kentucky militia

Colonel Pflueger (nf) – "Plug," keelboat captain and river pirate

Nine Eyes (nf) – Keelboat first mate and river pirate

General James Wilkinson (nf) – American general and adversary under Anthony Wayne, spy for Spain

Mrs. Pflueger (nf) – "Pluggy," wife of Colonel Pflueger and river pirate

Dalton brothers (nf) – River pirates

Chief Turkey Foot (nf) – "Men-sa-sa," Ottawa Indian chief resisting American expansion

Bad Bird (nf) – Chippewa Indian chief

Sauwaseekau (nf) – Tecumseh's Shawnee Indian brother

Tenskwatawa (nf) – "The Prophet," Tecumseh's Shawnee Indian brother

Quartermaster James O'Hara (nf) – Staff officer under Anthony Wayne during Fallen Timbers campaign, also called "Colonel" at times

Major Henry Burbeck (nf) – Artillery commander with Anthony Wayne, fort construction engineer

Lieutenant William Clark (nf) – Brother of George Rogers Clark, officer with Anthony Wayne's army legion, later was a part of Lewis and Clark exploration team

Ensign Meriwether Lewis (nf) – Served with Anthony Wayne and a part of the Lewis and Clark Exploration team

Brigadier General Thomas Posey (nf) – Officer during the Revolutionary War and Indian War, served with Anthony Wayne

Little Otter (nf) – Ottawa Indian chief

Bear King (nf) – Ottawa Indian chief

Chief Dog (nf) – Ottawa Indian chief

James Girty (nf) – Indian trader, brother of Simon and George

George Girty (nf) – Indian trader, brother of Simon and James

Chief Crane (nf) – Wyandotte Indian chief

Leather Lips (nf) – Wyandotte Indian chief

Black Tree (nf) – Kickapoo Indian chief

Dirty Face (nf) – Kickapoo Indian chief

Chief White Pigeon (nf) – Potawatomi Indian chief

Chief Big Cat (nf) – Delaware Indian chief

Lieutenant Tinsley (nf) – Commander of the rear guard flatboat of Anthony Wayne's flotilla

Captain Isaac Guion (nf) – Officer under James Wilkinson at Fort Washington

Major Thomas Cushing (nf) – Officer under General James Wilkinson

Piomingo (nf) – Chickasaw Indian chief

Chief Captain Pipe (nf) – Delaware Indian war chief

Sergeant Munson (nf) – Captured American soldier

Captain James Flinn (nf) – Head of a forty-man guide and scouting unit for General Wayne

Captain DeButts (nf) – Aide-de-camp for Anthony Wayne

Grey Wolf (F) – Miami Indian warrior, friend of Running Deer

General Charles Scott (nf) – Veteran of the French and Indian War and Revolutionary War, Kentucky militia leader during the Indian wars and future Governor of Kentucky

General Robert Todd (nf) – Served with Charles Scott and the Kentucky militia with Anthony Wayne

Lieutenant Robert Pilkington (nf) – British fort building engineer at Fort Miami

John Simcoe (nf) – Lt. Governor of Upper Canada

Ensign Dold (nf) – American spy and scout during the Anthony Wayne campaign

Captain William Eaton (nf) – Officer under Anthony Wayne

Captain Alexander Gibson (nf) – Commander at Fort Recovery during Indian siege there

Chief Bear (nf) – Northern Ottawa Indian chief

Major William McMahon (nf) – Frontiersman and scout hired by the U.S. government

Lieutenant Samuel Drake (nf) – Military officer at Fort Recovery

Captain Charles Beaubien (nf) – British leader at the Battle of Fort Recovery

Surgeon Mate James Andrews (nf) – Doctor at Fort Recovery during siege

Captain James Underwood (nf) – Interpreter for the Choctaw and Chickasaw Indians during Wayne campaign

James Donaldson (nf) – Indian interpreter for Anthony Wayne's legion

Chief Pipe (nf) – Delaware Indian chief

Christopher Miller (nf) – American spy and scout

Captain John Buell (nf) – Commander at Fort Greeneville during Wayne's absence

Ephraim Kibbey (nf) – Hired by Anthony Wayne to lead his famous forty scouts and spies

Major William Price (nf) – Leader of Anthony Wayne's legion advance guard

Robert Newman (nf) – American surveyor and then traitor

Lieutenant James Underhill (nf) – Commander left at outpost and supply station Fort Adams

Paschall Hickman (nf) – American scout and spy with William Wells

Chief Tarhe (nf) – Wyandotte Indian leader

Chief Black Hoof (nf) – Shawnee war chief

Major Thomas Hunt (nf) – Commander of Fort Defiance and later Fort Wayne during the 1800 building of the second Fort Wayne

George Schrim (nf) – American frontiersman and scout under Anthony Wayne

Captain Zebulon Pike (nf) – Commander at Fort Deposit during Fallen Timbers campaign and later a famous explorer

William May (nf) – Spy for Anthony Wayne captured and killed at Fallen Timbers

Captain Jacob Kingsbury (nf) – Commander of Anthony Wayne's 3rd Sub-legion at Fallen Timbers

Mr. Bevan (nf) – Captured British musician at Fort Miami during Fallen Timbers campaign

General Thomas Barbee (nf) – Kentucky militia general under Charles Scott at Fallen Timbers.

Deputy Sheriff Donnie Bork (F) Allen County (Indiana) Deputy Sheriff.

Chief of Police John Wynn (nf) – Fort Wayne, Indiana Chief of Police.

The Siege at Kekionga: Tecumseh's Uprising

Wayne Pastor Carlisle (F) – Son of E.J. and Charlotte Carlisle

Red Hawk (nf) – Miami Indian brave, son of Running Deer and Morning Bird

Louis Bourie (nf) – French businessman managing the portage between the St. Marys and Wabash rivers

Spotted Fawn (F) – Wife of Louis Bourie

Antoine Bondie (nf) – French trader and trapper at Kekionga

White Snake (F) – Wayne Pastor Carlisle's Indian name

Wy-nu-sa (F) – Miami Indian maiden at Hanging Rock, Red Hawk's love interest

Captain James Rhea (nf) – American commander at Fort Wayne during the 1812 Indian siege

Polly Rhea (nf) – Wife of Commander James Rhea of Fort Wayne

Toussaint Dubois (nf) – Scout and representative for William Henry Harrison

Lieutenant Phillip Ostrander (nf) – Officer at Fort Wayne during the 1812 siege and later temporary commander

John Johnston (nf) – Indian agent at Fort Wayne and later Piqua, Ohio

William Oliver (nf) – Assistant Indian agent at Fort Wayne

Colonel John Boyd (nf) – Officer under William Henry Harrison during Tippecanoe campaign

Abraham Owen (nf) – Aide-de-camp to William Henry Harrison during Tippecanoe campaign

John Chapman (nf) – "Johnny Appleseed," pioneer nurseryman orchardist, Swedenborgian New Church missionary and naturalist

Pechewa (nf) – "The Wildcat," Indian name of Jean Baptiste Richardville

Big Elk (F) – Potawatomi Indian brave and love interest of Wy-nu-sa at Hanging Rock

Maconaquah (nf) – Kidnapped as a 5-year-old white girl named Francis Slocum in Pennsylvania by Delaware Indians, she later became the wife of Miami Chief Shepocanah

Shepocanah (nf) – Miami war chief and husband of Maconaquah

Major Sam Wells (nf) – Kentucky militia officer and brother of William Wells

Mengoatawa (nf) – Kickapoo Indian war chief at Prophetstown

Wabaunsee (nf) – Potawatomi Indian war chief at Prophetstown

Waweapakoosa (nf) – Winnebago Indian war chief at Prophetstown

Roundhead (nf) – Wyandot Indian war chief at Prophetstown

Captain David Robb (nf) – Officer under Harrison at the Battle of Tippecanoe

Captain Spier Spencer (nf) – Leader of the "Yellow Jacket" militia from Harrison County, Indiana

Major Joseph Daviess (nf) – Dragoon leader under Harrison at the Battle of Tippecanoe

Rebekah Heald (nf) – Wife of Captain Nathan Heald (the commander at Fort Dearborn), niece of William Wells

Matthew Elliot (nf) – British Indian agent

Chief Metea (nf) – Potawatomi Indian chief on Cedar Creek, Allen County, Indiana

James Peltier (nf) – Early French pioneer at Kekionga

Chief Winamac (nf) – Potawatomi war chief

William Turner (nf) – Surgeon/doctor at 1812 Fort Wayne

Benjamin Stickney (nf) – Indian agent at 1812 Fort Wayne

Cut Finger (nf) – One of the two daughters of Maconaquah

Yellow Leaf (nf) – Youngest daughter of Maconaquah

Metocinyah (nf) – Miami Indian chief along Mississinewa River

Silver Heels (nf) – Miami Indian chief along the Mississinewa River

Francis Godfroy (nf) – Miami war chief

Private William Bailey (nf) – Soldier at 1812 Fort Wayne

Corporal Richards (nf) – Officer at 1812 Fort Wayne

Stephen Johnston (nf) – Assistant to Indian agent Benjamin Stickney and brother of John Johnston

Chief Coesse (nf) – Grandson of Chief Little Turtle

Pakoisheecan (nf) – Kickapoo war chief

Corporal Walter Jordan (nf) – Officer from Fort Wayne escorting William Wells to Fort Dearborn

Black Bird (nf) – Indian chief at 1812 Fort Dearborn

Nuscotnemeg (nf) – Indian chief at 1812 Fort Dearborn

Linai Helm (nf) – Lieutenant at 1812 Fort Dearborn

Captain Nathan Heald (nf) – U.S. Commander at 1812 Fort Dearborn

Black Partridge (nf) – Potawatomi chief at 1812 Fort Dearborn

Chandonnai (nf) – Half-breed Indian friendly to the Americans at 1812 Fort Dearborn

Margaret Helm (nf) – Wife of Lieutenant Linai Helm at Fort Dearborn

Captain Johnny Logan (nf) – "Spemica Lawba," Shawnee Indian spy who helped the American government

Peter Oliver (nf) – Fort Wayne resident who rode with Stephen Johnston in an effort to reach Piqua, Ohio

Five Medals (nf) – Potawatomi war chief helping to lead the siege at Fort Wayne

Bright Horn (nf) – Shawnee Indian spy partnered with Johnny Logan

Colonel John Allen (nf) – Militia officer from Kentucky under William Henry Harrison

Colonel William Lewis (nf) – Militia officer from Kentucky serving under Harrison

Colonel John Scott (nf) – Militia officer from Kentucky serving under Harrison

Reverend Matthew Wallace (nf) – Army chaplain for William Henry Harrison's army and first Presbyterian minister at 1812 Fort Wayne